UNDERCOVER LOVERS

The Trilogy

First published in 2018 by Sinful Press.
www.sinfulpress.co.uk
Copyright © 2017 Ellie Barker
Cover design by Studioenp

A CIP catalogue record for this book is available from the British Library

ISBN-13: 978-1-910908-28-0

UNDERCOVER LOVERS

The Trilogy

Ellie Barker

SINFUL PRESS

Contents

SECRETS & SPIES

IN BED WITH THE ENEMY

FOR QUEEN AND COUNTRY

BOOK ONE

SECRETS & SPIES

Chapter One

The first thing that attracted me to her was the bright blue, almost luminous hair. It's not often that you see a young woman with that particular shade of dye, and when you add chocolate skin it makes a rather arresting combination.

She was with another woman; tall with a long blonde plait, pale skin and dark eyes. She was pretty, sure, but fairly generic. I'd just come back from a stint in a place where beauty was in the unusual, and found that I'd gotten bored with standard looks. It takes something different to catch my eye, which Miss Blue-Hair provided. The hair drew my attention...and the rest of her kept it. Shorter than me—but then at over six foot, most people are. A slim body, from what I could see beneath her leather jacket. A tight ass beneath jeans that had holes in both knees. An effortless walk and a quick glance from dark eyes that seemed to take in every shadow and detail in seconds.

We were in a bar, and I admit I assumed she was there to do what everyone else was there to do—drink, flirt and forget about work. But as her friend found a willing target and homed in with a well-practiced flick of her hair, Miss Blue-Hair just found a table and pulled out her phone. Interesting.

Well, I can't say I'm averse to a challenge. I strolled over to Miss Blue-Hair, and her eyes flicked up to me as soon as I got within range. Maybe she was on the pull after all. I met her eyes and smiled, gesturing to the seat opposite her. "May I?"

She gave me an assessing look, and I wondered what she thought of me. Six-foot-something with dark hair tied into a ponytail, bright blue eyes and a lean face, mostly consisting of planes and angles. As her eyes scanned down my body and back up, I resisted the urge to smirk. Nice muscles covered by jeans and a black t-shirt that had short enough arms to show off those muscles; I say it myself, but I look good. Obviously, she approved, because she nodded towards the empty space. "Of course."

I slid into the seat and grinned. "I would ask what a nice girl like you is doing in a place like this, but…"

"I'm not a nice girl." I saw the glint in her eyes, and then a real smile curved her mouth as she saw that I got the joke. She had a faint accent, and to my ear it was hella sexy. "What's your name?"

"Nikolas. Yours?" I prompted when all I got was a faint frown.

"Sky."

That took a moment to sink in. "Fucking hell, *the* Sky?"

She rolled her eyes and leaned back. "Which stories have

you heard?"

"The thief."

"You've still got all of your valuables, right?"

"So far."

"You've been here for a few seconds. You're safe."

"I wouldn't say that." I smirked at her.

That made her grin and lean forward again. "All right. You want to fuck me?"

I couldn't help the laugh. I liked her. "It had crossed my mind."

She took a sip of her drink, and casually said, "So how many ways do you swing?"

It took me a moment to catch on, I admit, and I think my eyebrows went up. She was slim, sure, and now that I noticed there wasn't any bust beneath that leather jacket. But she'd moved like a dancer, and I'd sure as hell not have suspected anything if she hadn't hinted.

She was waiting for me to react, but hey, I've lived with surprises for long enough that nothing really phases me. I grinned. "I'm a bit out of practise, but I've always got time for re-learning."

She—he?—returned the grin, eyes flashing with amusement. "All right. Drink?"

"Water."

That made…let's go with 'her'…eyebrows go up. "Just once or is that a habit?"

"Habit."

She shrugged. "Come and loom over the bar, then. You'll get the barman's attention."

I took advantage of the pause as we were leaning there,

waiting for drinks. "All right, so just to get this straight…" No one can accuse me of being subtle. "Are you a man or a woman?"

"Male genitals, but female pronouns." She'd obviously been asked enough times, and she had a steely glint in her eye. "Good enough?"

I can't resist an opening like that. "I dunno, you haven't proved that yet."

She had the dirtiest laugh that I've heard for a while, and that was the point I decided I was taking her home. If any woman laughs like that to one of my bad jokes, then I'm doing everything in my power to get her into bed. It's a policy that's earned me most of my best nights.

We had a few drinks and then she made sure her friend was set, slung her jacket back on, and gave me the most come-hither look I've seen in a long time. I walked her back to mine, trading insults the entire way and getting quite a few more laughs. She made me laugh too, which was a pleasure. I didn't get a lot of answers out of her, but then to be fair, I didn't really answer any questions either. We reached a mutual understanding—the first of several that evening, I admit.

I escorted her in to my apartment on the ground floor of a faded, elegant stone building, and after she 'd declined a drink and poked around briefly, I steered her into the bedroom. That was when I got my second surprise of the evening.

She'd undressed, and I was admiring her from behind, enjoying the faint curve of her hips and her definitely gropeable buttocks…I might have tested that on the way home. But it was as she stepped back and raised her arms above her head, lifting her bright blue hair, that I realised I'd seen her before.

She'd had shorter hair, then, as black as night. She'd been dressed in practical trousers and a t-shirt, and carrying a bag full of tools; an electrician's apprentice, fixing lights in an office building. They'd been in and out before anyone had realised some rather valuable documents had been copied and somehow removed from the building despite the security.

I'd idly wondered if the maintenance crew I'd walked past had been involved. After all, it wasn't a dissimilar cover to one that I'd occasionally employed for jobs...

Sky. Thief, seductress, gambler and heartbreaker. This slim, dark-eyed thing in my bed was that legend.

Well, I can't refuse a chance to fuck a legend. I'd just have to discuss her previous activities with her when we'd finished this business.

That train of thought came to a very nice conclusion as she turned to me, lifting her arms and stretching, taking my open mouth and caught breath as appreciation. "Lost for words?"

I managed a smile. "I've never been one for talking when I could express my appreciation in...other ways."

She fitted perfectly across my hips, her strong legs pressing on my thighs. I felt her cock slide against my stomach, leaving a wet trail in contrast to the warmth of the smooth skin. Her mouth pressed onto mine as I pulled her closer, and we spent a while like that, chests pushed together and skin sliding as my hands explored her body and her tongue teased mine, her long fingers winding into my hair.

"All right, enough," I said when it got too distracting, pushing her shoulders back a little to get some distance. "I want in you."

Her mouth twitched into a smile. "Condom?"

"Always to hand." I put my arm behind my back and pulled one from under the pillow. "You or me?"

"As you asked so nicely, I figure I should let you fuck me." Sky has a certain turn of phrase, and in that case, it was a turn-on phrase. I was hard already but that just put the edge on it.

The condom was cool against my hot skin, and as Sky stayed where she was, it meant I was touching us both as I rolled it on. She seemed to like my hands against her, and I took a moment to stroke up her cock where it rested against my stomach.

"C'mon," she told me, her voice wavering into a groan for a moment. "Lube?"

I found that under the pillow, too, much to her amusement.

"What else you got under there?" she asked.

"Hang around and you might find out." I liked the way her mouth twitched when she was amused, and took a minute to kiss it as I smeared lube on my cock.

We were still mouth-to-mouth as I tipped her backwards onto the bed, her legs still against my thighs and my arms around her back. It put my lubed cock in the perfect spot to slide down between her ass cheeks and press against her.

"Do it…" the husky voice said into my hair, and I felt her yield as I pushed against her tight circle. Slowly, that was the way, gentle and slow even though what I really wanted to do was bury myself inside her…

She was good, I'll give her that. A few strokes and she was relaxing around me, and then her legs shifted to wrap around my back and she'd pulled me to her in one swift, unexpected movement. My hands tightened on her shoulders and I swore into her neck as she took my length, still so tight that I could feel her ring gripping at the base of my cock. It was probably the most intense thing I'd ever experienced, and I nearly came right then.

She kept me for a moment, legs tight around my back. I slid my hands up to her bright hair and pulled her head back a little, biting at her neck, trying to make her twitch. When she did, I could feel the movement all the way down her body.

"Bastard," she murmured to me, and I felt her legs loosen a little. "You feel good."

"So...do...you..." I told her, matching the words to slow strokes and seeing her eyes start to unfocus, her hands grasping my shoulders. I pushed myself up a little and stopped for a moment.

"You...ok?" she asked, refocusing on me.

"Just..." I paused, and then reached forward and lightly brushed a curled strand of hair away from her eyes. "Just adding something."

The handful of lube was cold on my palm, but when I wrapped it around her cock I was rewarded with a convulsive spasm and a low moan as I ran my hand down the length and then up again. "Oh, fuck..."

"Absolutely." I snagged one of her hands and, wrapping her fingers around her own cock, slid both of my hands down her body as I admired her slender chest. There was barely any change of shape between her ribs and stomach and hips, the bones all protruding ever-so-slightly under the muscle. My hands stopped at the top of her legs and then I was moving again, shifting my hips backward and forward, pushing into her. I was rewarded with a moan and her legs tightening around me, and her hand started to move.

She matched her strokes to mine and I felt her entire body open to me as I increased my speed. My own pleasure was taking over and I don't think I could have slowed down, wanting the next thrust and the next and next—

She moved her thumb up to the head of her shaft and a moment later was twitching, gasping, and everything tensed around me as a stream of white shot across her stomach and chest. That was enough to push me over the edge—well, I'd been close for a while. I left bruises on her thighs from my hands as I came, and I probably swore. I try to mind my language a little, but that was intense.

When I opened my eyes, I was looking down at her face, framed with that bright blue hair. Her eyes opened a moment later, lazily, and then focused on me as a smile twitched at her lips. "Nice."

"Agreed." I felt my thigh muscles protest as I shifted back and then started to withdraw. She released her legs from around my back and looked around for a tissue as I pulled my condom off.

"Here," I told her, and snagged the box from the side of the bed. Hey, I like to be prepared.

We both cleaned ourselves up, and then looked at each other, sat on the edge of the bed. I think that set the tone; neither of us seemed to be particularly cuddly people. But I ran my hand down a strand of that hair and then across the wet lips, and got a smile.

"So," I said conversationally. "Gonna tell me what you did with the documents you stole?"

I'll give her credit; she didn't flinch. I was expecting her to try to run, but she just gave me a thoughtful look, tinged with a certain amount of amusement. This was a game, and she was playing. "You'll have to be more specific, Nikolas."

I liked the way she pronounced my name; she gave it the correct harshness of the *k* and some length on the *a*. "You were an electrician, and then just after you'd vanished, some documents were also found to have vanished." My fingers returned to her hair and wove into the bright strands. "You were dark then."

And before she could answer, before she could lie to me, I tightened my grip and dipped my head to her exposed neck.

"And don't think," I added, feeling my lips move against her skin, "of lying."

"But if I lie," Sky's breathy voice said from somewhere by my ear, "you'd just have to get the truth out of me, wouldn't you?"

"How would I do that?" I let my teeth enclose a bite of skin, with enough pressure to tell her that I could make a mark if I wanted to.

"You don't know how to?"

My teeth did leave a mark, white on her dark skin, and she groaned. I felt one of her hands come around my back and the other trail up my leg, towards my now-stiffening cock.

"But the problem with this," I said, and left another mark on her neck, "is that you like it."

"If you're nice to me—" Another groan as my teeth bit in again. "Maybe I'll tell you the truth."

I trailed my tongue down her neck, keeping my hand entwined in her hair. Her hands were now doing interesting things to my shoulders and back. "How nice would I have to be?" I asked when I'd finished with that patch of skin.

"Very."

With one movement I pulled her across my lap, her chest against my bare thighs. One of my hands was still wound in her hair, and her buttocks were lying just in the path of my other hand.

I gave her a moment to anticipate what was about to happen, and then I brought my palm down sharply.

Sky groaned, and I felt her cock twitch against my leg. When her voice came, it had the delicious hitch of someone hovering between pleasure and pain. "That's not nice."

"No." I punctuated the word with another slap. "It's not."

She was gasping and I felt her thrust her hips against me as I spanked her again. She wasn't even trying to fight; one hand was wound under my legs and the other pushed against my calf, and she was almost rock-hard now. I was, too; the way she moved on my lap was infuriating.

I spanked her until she was moaning under me, begging me to stop and please just fuck her again. But I slid my hand across her burning skin and smiled as she panted. "You were going to tell me some secrets."

"Fuck me."

"And you'll tell me?"

"Yes."

I unwound my hand from her hair and pulled her upright, back to where she had been sitting, and then promptly pushed her back onto the rumpled sheets. She went back onto her elbows, wincing as the fabric moved under her sore buttocks. "What now?"

I found a condom and rolled it on to her cock, and then shifted myself to kneel between her thighs and pulled her forward by her hips, sliding my cool hands under her ass.

"I'm going to be nice to you. And you're going to talk."

Her dark eyes were watching me as I lowered my head and gently licked the tip of her cock. The way she shuddered told me she was just as turned on as I was. Not that the rock-hard cock in front of me was disagreeing with that summary.

"I am an electrician. We did the work."

I slid my tongue down her shaft and back up, and felt her shudder again as I flicked the top.

"I knew of the documents."

Her cock fitted into my mouth, but I made the descent slow, tantalising.

"I...didn't...steal...them..."

Back up and down again, swirling my tongue around the head as I came up, feeling it jerk in my mouth.

"I carried...I carried them. We were there...and could take them out."

I was moving faster, letting her hips move in my hands, pushing her up towards me as my mouth slid down her cock.

"I knew they...were important. But I didn't...steal. Not that time."

She was still lubed from earlier, and I freed a thumb to slide into her asshole. The thrust of pleasure nearly made me choke. Good thing I'm still ok at deep-throating.

I pulled out and teased the tip of her cock with my lips, raising my eyes to see the desperate face framed by bright blue hair, body tense with desire and need.

"That's all. I swear. I swear—"

And she did swear for real as I lowered my head again, plunging my thumb in and out of her ass as I let my mouth do the work. It was only a few seconds before her body jerked and tensed under me, and she made the most adorable deep groan as she came.

As she relaxed, I slid my hands out and gave the tip of her cock a final flick with my tongue that made her twitch.

"You," she told me, opening her eyes, "are very good at that."

"I'll start advertising as a professional torturer."

That got a smile, and then abruptly she pushed herself up. "You. On the bed."

I smiled, but I wasn't going to disobey. "What do I have to tell you?"

"Why were you there?" She knelt between my legs and grabbed the lube. As her hands stroked up and down my cock, I wondered how the hell she'd even been able to talk while I was blowing her. I was *so* turned on.

"Business. Same kind. You nicked the documents before I could."

She laughed, and then I swore and lost track of time for a bit. When I came back from that intense burst of pleasure, she was still there, kneeling naked between my thighs. "Who wanted them?"

"The highest bidder," I managed.

She snorted and climbed off. "Big shots with too much money."

"Who did you give them to?"

She gave me a long look, and then a smile. "The Queen."

I admit I was surprised that she'd told me, but hey, don't

look a gift horse in the cock. I leaned myself up on one elbow and smiled back at her. "So, now we've got that little confessional out the way…wanna come back sometime?"

She made a face, but her eyes were glinting in amusement. "Leave the money on the dresser?"

"You know it." I grinned at her. "I'm just gonna pee, so back in a minute."

That was when I learned something about Sky. I didn't take long to pee, but when I came out, she'd gone. Clothes gone, jacket off the hook, front door shut; and she'd done it absolutely silently.

I had opened my mouth to swear when I spotted something. A white card, left on the hall table that's probably the closest thing I have to a dresser. Written on it was a mobile number, and the message "Call me." And then a scrawled, "S".

I held the card between two fingers, smiling down at it. That was one intriguing woman, and the sex…well, it was good. Possibly even great.

Chapter Two

I called her the next day.

Hey, I had to leave time for my muscles to recover a bit.

She picked up on the second ring. "*Hello?*"

"I want to meet the Queen."

"*And here I was thinking you wanted a date*," Sky's voice said from the other end of the line. I was leaning against a wall, watching people hurry past me. It was drizzling slightly, so no one was really paying much attention.

"I'd like a date," I told the amused woman on the phone, "but I want to see her too."

"*You ask so nicely. Thursday. 8pm. The Roadkill Bar.*"

"Wait, I'm busy—"

She'd already hung up on me. I swore. Thursday, I *was* busy, but…well. Looked like I'd have to get un-busy.

So, on Thursday at 8pm I was at the Roadkill. It was filled

with a fair share of degenerates, and I certainly looked in place amongst them. I got some chips and a pint of water, and propped up the bar while wondering where my date was.

By the time half an hour had passed I was wondering if this was a set-up. The research I'd done suggested that it wasn't…well, that this pub was legitimate, at least. My being here, not so much.

Sky wandered in about fifteen minutes later, just as I was debating whether to give up and accept that I'd been screwed. She gave me a smile that made me forgive her every minute of my wait, and grabbed my hand. "C'mon. I'll take you someplace better."

I followed obediently and we headed through a door in the back of the pub. It looked like it led to the toilets, which it did —and another door, with a wide flight of stairs.

"Didn't realise this place had a cellar," I commented.

Sky just shrugged.

"Not revealing trade secrets, eh?"

"You haven't done anything to get them out of me."

I hadn't spotted any cameras, so I leaned forward to put my lips by her ear. "I'll start a list."

"That sounds fun." Her voice dropped into a husky note, and my cock twitched. I really liked this girl.

The stairs led to a corridor with a couple of doors. Sky walked to the end and knocked. After a moment, a voice said, "Yes?"

"I brought Nikolas," Sky said, opening the door.

I followed her in to a large office. There was an open door at the far end, leading to what looked like another corridor. The office itself had a polished meeting table to one side and a desk on the other, complete with a shiny computer screen. It was smart, modern—despite the rather worn grey carpet—and mostly eclipsed by the woman walking around the desk to meet us.

She wasn't beautiful, but she was noticeable. She had high cheekbones and a thin nose, which I felt really should have had glasses on. A blouse revealed cleavage that I suspected was helped by a push-up bra, and the brown skirt clung just enough to reveal toned thighs. I'd have estimated her at late thirties or mid-forties; no grey hair, but enough lines to suggest she'd seen a lot.

"Sky. This is your latest catch?" I got the most judging look I'd ever received, and then the woman turned back to Sky. "Is he any good?"

"Business, he's competent. Sex, he's good." And then Sky laughed and amended, "With my body. With yours, I don't know."

The Queen turned her eyes back to me. "So?"

"I'm after some documents—"

"I know." She was eyeing me frankly. "I want a sweetener. If Sky says you're good, I want proof."

I managed to shut my mouth before I gaped. "I don't usually allow try before you buy, ma'am."

"But for me, you'll make an exception." She beckoned. "Come here."

I swallowed, and made one of the split-second decisions that seemed to characterise my life. This was another game, and I was playing. "Yes, ma'am."

I walked towards her, and stopped a few steps away from the side of the desk.

"So?"

The door to one side was open a little, but I couldn't spot anyone watching. Sky was still in the room anyway, now with her bum on the conference table and her arms folded, smiling faintly. So...what the hell.

I took the remaining two steps to the Queen and pushed her backwards gently, until her ass was against the edge of the desk. A quick movement to slide her skirt up, a lift of her thighs to get them open, and I went straight in.

Well, metaphorically. Actually, I dallied. I licked and teased and circled and teased again, and just as I could feel her breathing quicken, slid two fingers into her wet cunt. Her thighs tensed against my shoulders and I curled my fingers, rubbing the wall before sliding out again and repeating.

It went down well. Just as I'd moved on to sucking at her clit, she groaned and orgasmed. Luckily she wasn't a squirter; I wasn't in a particularly good position for that surprise. Not that I necessarily mind, just there's a time and a place.

I pulled my fingers out, sucked them clean and got myself off my knees. Hopefully that would win me the first round of the game...

"So," the Queen said, sitting up. The business-like tone surprised me; the only thing that suggested she'd just had an orgasm was the flush on her cheeks and the slightly quicker breathing. I was impressed. "You want something."

I wiped my mouth and sat in the nearest chair as the Queen sat back down behind the desk, looking thoroughly composed. "I want to know who the documents were passed on to, or copies of them."

"Why?"

"Because I've got a buyer and Sky's team put the wind up the source."

Out of the corner of my eye, I noticed Sky make a face at me.

"What's your price for copies?"

"Give me some sort of ballpark," I complained. "My buyers aren't millionaires, so if that's the level I'll just explore other options."

The Queen gave an amused huff. "Ten thousand, because I like you."

I gave her my nicest smile. "Would you take five?"

"Ten thousand, or explore your other methods."

"I'll pass it on." I stood and held out a hand. "Nice to have met you, ma'am."

"I'll let you know if I have a use for you." But she did smile as she shook my hand, and I followed Sky back out of the room.

***

"Who did they get delivered to?" I asked Sky as we went back down the corridor.

"Looking for a cheaper price? Not gonna tell you."

"Do I have to persuade you again?"

She turned around and grinned at me. "Won't work."

We were climbing the steps again and I grabbed her belt, shoving her against the wall and stepping up to the same level as I did so. My head was above hers, and the handrail pushed her hips out, forcing her crotch against mine. I looked down at that bright blue hair and shining eyes. "Really? Not even if I offered you something in return?"

"Depends what you're offering."

I leaned down and kissed her, pushing my tongue into her mouth. She returned the kiss with passion, and I felt movement against my jeans. My own cock was rising too. "Information," I said when we finally parted. "Something for something. You tell me something, I tell you something." I pushed my lips against her ear, and said, "Documents, buyer."

She considered it as she ran her hand down my back, flattening my t-shirt against my skin. "I'm interested. But you could just tell me they like chocolate."

"I don't know if they do, actually," I confessed, slightly distracted. Her hand had slipped under my t-shirt and was sliding up my back, cool against my skin. "I've never asked."

"Maybe we should find somewhere more private to discuss this."

"I don't know, I like it here."

It was hard, fast, rough sex; Sky kneeling on the grey carpet in front of me with her jeans pulled down, my hands pinning hers against the worn fabric, my cock thrusting into her tight ass. She felt damn good, and she obviously liked it.

I came with a groan and leaned against her for a moment, panting. "You didn't finish. Wanna take this someplace else so I can rectify that?"

She shivered as I withdrew. "You can owe me."

"Sure?"

I saw the grin. "Hell yeah."

"You're on." I pulled the condom off and found a tissue. "Well, I gotta go phone people."

"Add me to the list." She pulled up her jeans, gave me a wink, and then we carried on up the stairs as if nothing had happened.

***

It was twenty-three hours later when I got a call.

"*Date night?*" Sky asked.

"I'm busy," I complained. I was. I had a rather cute blonde waiting for me and much as I wanted to fuck Sky again, I didn't want to end up too interested in her.

"*I've got a present for you.*"

"Can't you just give it to me?"

She snorted. "*Kiss and run, sure. Tell you what, I'll leave it with your date.*"

"How did you know—" But she'd hung up, and didn't pick up when I called back.

Over dinner, my date did give me the files—or at least, handed over a small USB with a smile. "A friend said you wanted this?"

"Friend?"

"Blue hair."

"Yeah. You know her?"

The woman shrugged. "Business."

I resisted the urge to roll my eyes. Well, that was clear. And it also meant that I wasn't going to risk taking this woman back to my place. Instead, I opted for a hotel, and the night was ok, but I didn't enjoy it as much as I should have. Dark skin, lean hips and bright blue hair kept intruding into my thoughts, and by daybreak I was grouchy, despite having sated my urges several times.

I dropped my date off, got myself a coffee, and irritably took the USB stick off to someone who would know what to do with it. I needed it checked before it went to my buyers.

***

I got the call at 2am. I was, incidentally, awake, but still had to rub my eyes to see who was calling. Benny. My resident computer geek and partner in crime. "Yeah?"

"*They're encrypted. Where's the key?*"

"You can't decrypt them?"

"*Not without a supercomputer.*"

"Fuck. I'll see what I can do."

"*Oh,*" Benny added as I was about to hang up. "*They had a virus protecting them too. Nasty little thing. Impressive.*"

Benny doesn't call something impressive unless he means it. "What did it do?"

"*Rogue hacker. Would have sent information to whoever's on the other end. Someone doesn't trust you.*"

"You nuked it?"

"*Of course.*" Benny sounded offended.

"I'll get you the key."

He hung up on me.

So. I now had to get an encryption key. And I knew who to call.

Chapter Three

It wasn't hard. As Sky walked in the front door of my place after a few drinks at my local bar, I shut the door with one foot and slammed her into the wall, hands over her head. "What's the key?"

"I don't know it." She managed wide-eyed innocence, but she wasn't surprised. She knew where this was going.

I grabbed both her wrists with one hand and pushed the other up her neck, tilting her head back. "You know it. Tell me."

I wasn't really angry. I wasn't going to force her. She knew that.

But boy, was it fun to play.

"Or what?" The eyes that looked up at me were bright. She was enjoying this just as much as I was.

"I make you tell me."

"Bring it on." And the bitch slid her foot around my ankle and kicked my leg out from under me.

I landed on one knee on the floor, letting go of her arms as I did so, more shocked that she'd got one over on me than actually hurt. But I was still quick enough to snag her leg as she darted away and promptly sent her crashing to the floor, too. Then it was a simple enough matter to get myself on top of her.

"You're not too good at this, are you?" she told me. I could feel her body pressing against me, her cock a pulsing bulge against my hip. Her lips were just there, waiting to be kissed.

I bit her bottom lip instead.

She gasped and I felt her entire body tense against mine.

My hand caught her wrist as she went to slap my ass, and slammed it into the floor above her head. The other one followed.

"Good enough," I told her, pinning both wrists with one hand again. The other snaked down her chest and found a nipple through the fabric of her shirt, gently circling as it rose. And then I pinched, hard.

She gasped again.

I lowered my head to her ear and bit. A shiver, this time; one I could feel all the way down her skin.

"Want more?" I murmured into her ear, feeling her blue hair smooth against my nose.

"Yes." It was more moan than word.

My bites trailed down her neck and then I pushed myself up, grinding her wrists into the floor. My knees went between her thighs and pushed them open. Hell, she was beautiful, spread out beneath me, her shirt riding up her stomach and the bulge of her cock distorting her jeans.

"I could take you, here," I told her. "On the cold floor, naked. Force you to do what I want."

Her wide eyes were staring up at me, and I saw the bulge in her jeans twitching. I lowered my mouth to her ear again. "I'd fuck you. Here. Ride you. Make you scream."

"Do it." It was another moan. "Please. Do it."

My hand gently trailed down her chest and popped the jeans buttons, slid the zip down. She wasn't wearing underwear, and her cock slid easily out of the gap. "You want me to fuck you."

"Yes."

I let one finger slide across the tip, feeling the dampness, and then raised it to her lips for her to suck. "You want me to push you down, thrust myself into you, fuck you so hard you're screaming…"

"Yes!"

I leaned down again, my hand still grasping her wrists above her head, her body so beautifully stretched under mine. "No."

She moaned. "Please."

"You're going to be my toy."

"Yes. Yes, please."

"You're going to get up, get undressed, go and lie on the bed. I'm going to watch you."

"Yes."

"Yes, what?"

"Yes, sir."

I let her wrists go and got off her. "Go on."

I followed her as she went into the bedroom, and caught

the look in her eyes as she glanced back to check I was following. She was enjoying this as much as I was. There was even a faint smile lingering on her lips.

She pulled her shirt off, letting it linger above her head. And then slid the jeans down.

And then she lay down on the bed, and watched me.

I smiled at her. "You're going to be my fuck toy, Sky. You're going to put your hands above your head and hold on to those bars, and you're not going to let go. Is that clear? Or do I have to find a restraint?"

That brought a moment of doubt and fear, and she shook her head. "No. I'll stay."

I nodded, and pulled my own shirt off. As she slid her hands up and took hold of the bedframe, I pulled my own jeans down and then my boxers, shivering for a moment in the sudden cold.

Then I found the lube and a condom and walked across to the bed, aware of Sky's eyes on me. Her skin was starting to chill in the colder air, but her cock was still erect. I think she was enjoying the sight. Well, I hope she was.

I rolled the condom onto her cock without any other foreplay, feeling her twitch, and then gently ran lube down it. She was watching, hands grasping the bars.

I settled myself over her body, and leaned forward to kiss a nipple. The change from cold to the warmth of my mouth made her gasp again, and I felt the cold of the lube against my leg as her cock twitched under me.

"Hold still," I told her, and gently started to push onto her.

She grasped the bars but did hold still as I slowly opened

my ass, pushing in little by little. It was fun for me but torment for her, feeling me tight around the head of her cock and wanting to be further inside. But she stayed still.

"Good girl," I told her, leaning forward to kiss her. As her tongue wound against mine I slid a little further down her cock and felt her body tense as she moaned. "Now, what have you got to tell me?"

"Ask."

"The encryption. I need a key."

"Yes."

It was obvious now why she had told me about the documents so quickly, and why the Queen had given them to me. They were useless without the key. I slid a little further down Sky's cock and then back up again. "You didn't give me the key."

Her eyes glinted. She might be desperately wanting me to fuck her, but she still had smarts. "You didn't ask."

"Oh, dear." I slid a hand up her body and pinched her nipple hard. She jerked under me, body writhing.

"It's separate," she gasped out. "They did it like that."

"So, what is the key? Do you know it?"

"No. It's a computer key."

I abruptly slid down on her cock, pushing her all the way in. Her body arched, and the most delicious low moan came from her lips. "Ohhhh."

"That's what you get for being a good girl," I told her, trying not to smile at the words. Oh, the games we play… "So how do I get a copy of this key?"

"The Queen's got one."

I stayed where I was and brought my hand to my own

cock, starting to stroke. I could see Sky's chest move as she felt my muscles contract. "And how do I get it from the Queen?"

Sky's hands were still clenched around the bars of my bedframe, but she grinned at me, suddenly looking amused. The game had been put aside for a moment. "Was there a virus on the documents?"

I sat still for a moment, just looking at her. "Yes."

"Hm. She doesn't like you that much, then. You'd have to give her something."

I released my cock and leaned forward. "Something. What kind of thing?"

"She'd like it if you fucked her. Beyond that, I'm not sure what she wants." Sky's expression was half mocking, half serious. "You'd have to ask her."

"You'll take me to see her again."

"Maybe." A pinch of her other nipple made her writhe again. "Still maybe."

And I sat back up, smiling. "All right."

I kept her under me, her cock twitching inside me, and brought myself to a long, slow orgasm that was one of the most satisfying I've had in years. Sky was moaning under me as I came all over her chest, swearing out my own pleasure.

I opened my eyes, and gave her another smile. "That's me. Now you."

And I used her. I rode her slowly, gently, bringing her so close to climax and then stopping, leaving her swearing and begging. I fucked her until I'd recovered and could play with myself again, sending more liquid to join the drying mess on her stomach. She was gripping the bedframe, desperately thrusting her hips up, begging me to just fuck her, just let her come, please…

I leaned forward, feeling the tired glow of the orgasms and the hardness of her in my ass. "What are you going to do for me?"

"I'll take you to see her."

"And the encryption?"

She was panting.

"You'll help me get it. You won't trick me."

"I don't know what she wants for it."

"You'll help me."

"Yes. I'll help you. Yes, yes, yes—"

And she came as I fucked her hard, her hands so tight on the bedframe that her knuckles were white, her blue hair spilling around her head, body arching.

I slid off as she relaxed, and sat down next to her as she opened her eyes.

"You bastard."

"You know, you could have just told me all of that at the start," I protested mildly.

"It wouldn't have been nearly as much fun."

I looked at her; red-faced, sweaty, lying on stained and crumpled bedsheets. "Good point."

Sky stretched languidly. "So," she said. "When do you wanna see her?"

"When I've had a shower." I ran a hand down her sweaty, beautiful body. "Come and have one too, then I know you won't run out on me again."

She swung her legs off the bed with a grin. "Yes, sir."

***

We went back to the bar, and down to the cellar. I admit that my nerves were screaming at me; it felt like a trap. I was at the mercy of someone who had already lied to me, but...

Well. Let's just say that my hormones were doing half the talking, and the rest of my brain really wanted to know who'd screwed me over—and tried to get a virus onto Benny's computer. Gits.

I know that sort of thing is done, but call me old-fashioned, I like the standard tail-and-chase-'em. It gives me something to dodge. None of this damn computer stuff.

But that's why I have Benny on my side.

We headed down the back steps again, and I felt Sky's hand linger on my ass. I smiled down at her, remembering fucking her on the stairs. She was certainly intriguing.

Maybe that was the point.

Was she a set-up, too?

Sky knocked on the door, and I heard a muffled voice. We entered.

The Queen was there, sitting behind the desk, and gave a brief smile as I entered behind Sky. "Nikolas."

"I need the key." I couldn't be bothered to be subtle. She'd given me the documents; she'd know what I'd come back for.

"That's got a higher price."

I gave her a long stare. "Two orgasms?" I asked snarkily.

"Indeed."

I hesitated. I'd been joking, but that had been too easy. "Well? Do I get details before I agree?"

"I'm going to watch."

I just looked at her.

"And film it."

"No."

"You can have a mask, dear boy."

"No." I folded my arms. "I'm not stupid enough to give you blackmail material."

"But you'd let me watch."

I managed a shrug. "If that's what gets you off, why do I care? Who do you want me to fuck?"

The Queen raised a hand, and pointed at one of the burly thugs standing at the side of the room. "He's going to fuck your smart mouth."

I swallowed. "And the other one?"

"Will be much more pleasurable, I assure you. Two orgasms, no filming. Is that fair?"

I bit down nerves, and nodded.

"There's no cameras in here," the Queen said, and raised a hand. "Pat, come here." The burly man was only slightly taller than me, but a good half as wide again. "You may come in this man's mouth."

The burly man nodded, pulled a condom out of his pocket, and undid his jeans.

"On your knees," the Queen purred to me.

Now, I'm definitely a top. I don't get off on pain unless I'm inflicting it, and then only when my partner's enjoying it. Tears definitely aren't my thing.

But that was the point.

It was fast and hard; luckily I'm good at deep-throating, so it wasn't particularly painful. I'm sure if I'd begged he would have stopped—but that was the point. This wasn't what I'd have picked as a fun sexual encounter, but I was damned if I was going to give up in front of her.

I think the tears that coated my cheeks as I gagged on his

cock gave her enough pleasure. I caught her smiling, and then he was plunging in and out, and all I could focus on was getting him off as fast as possible while resisting the urge to gag when his cock filled my throat. It was a mercifully short time later when I felt him spasm and had to force back the urge to vomit. I'd never been so grateful for that thin piece of latex separating the two of us.

My jaw hurt when he withdrew, and I wiped my cheeks with the back of my hand. "Now what, ma'am?"

"You can please Sky. In front of me," the Queen said, smiling again.

Well, that would be a lot more pleasurable...but did involve someone else. I stood up and walked over to where Sky was standing, suddenly looking nervous. I touched her shoulder, and she turned. "Are you going to obey me?" I asked quietly.

I saw nervousness briefly cross her face, and she looked into my eyes. I don't know what she saw there, but she nodded, and even managed a brief smile.

I smiled back, and gently kissed her.

Showtime.

I turned Sky and walked her to stand directly in front of the woman sitting in the chair, whose eyes were fixed on us even though her expression was almost one of boredom. I felt Sky shaking as I undid her jeans, but her cock was erect as soon as my hand stroked up it. I slid her jeans down, exposing those gropeable buttocks, and then pulled the t-shirt up.

"Off," I told her.

She obediently kicked her shoes off, let the jeans fall, and pulled her arms up so I could strip her t-shirt over her head.

She was still shaking. She didn't know what I was going to do, and I liked that. But by the way she moved for me, she liked it too—and her erect cock told me that she was definitely getting off on it.

The Queen was still watching me, despite the naked body in front of her. I pushed Sky to her knees, and bent to place one of her hands on each of the Queen's knees so that she was leaning forward, exposed for me to fuck. "There," I told her. "Stay."

Her cock was still hard, pulsing. I lingered for a minute to trace my tongue down Sky's neck, feeling the Queen's eyes on the little tableau that was playing out right in front of her. Sky's naked form almost between her legs, my clothed one behind her, in control...

I slowly undid my own jeans and pulled my cock out. The Queen's eyes lingered on that, and her tongue slowly licked wet lips as I pulled a condom out of my pocket and rolled it on.

"I could use some lube," I told the Queen.

She lifted a hand and waved it to someone behind me. "In the desk drawer."

The burly thug came over a few seconds later with a small bottle. I gave him a smile. "Thanks."

"Welcome." He lingered for a moment, eyes on my cock and Sky's naked back, and then he retreated again.

I traced a hand down Sky's back, and then into the crack of her ass. I followed it with a trail of lube, and saw her twitch at the cold. She twitched again as I followed the trail with a finger, and then gave a low moan as I gently pushed my thumb into her ass.

The Queen smiled, and leaned back to get a better view. I reached up with my free hand and wound a hand into Sky's hair, pulling her head back so that her face would be visible to the woman in front of her.

"Very nice," the Queen said as I withdrew my thumb and pushed it in again, making Sky's body twitch. "You know how to please me, Nikolas."

"Do you want me to continue?" I pulled my thumb out again and ran it gently around the rim of Sky's anus, making her moan again.

"Slowly."

"As the Queen commands."

And I went slowly. I teased and tormented Sky until she forgot that she was kneeling in a cold room in front of her boss, forgot that she was naked in a roomful of people, forgot everything except my cock in her ass and my hand on her shaft. I fucked her until she was begging and then gave the Queen a raised eyebrow.

The woman nodded. "She may come."

And Sky bucked and cried out as I plunged into her again and again.

When the spasm was over and her head was hanging, her body exhausted, I slowly withdrew. I hadn't come, but I think that was also the point.

The Queen smiled, and nodded as Sky looked up. "Very nice. Get cleaned up, Sky, and then take Nikolas to have a drink. On my tab."

I guessed this was some sort of favour, and Sky nodded. I gave her my hand as she stood up, and got a grateful twitch of her mouth as her legs shook under her. She had the faintly dazed expression of someone who'd just been thoroughly blissed out. "Shower. This way."

***

Half an hour later, we were ordering drinks upstairs. Sky had shaken her head at my suggestion of going back to the flat, and I guessed that we had to stay until we got an answer. I was feeling like I'd just had an exam, and was waiting nervously for marks. Would that be enough? Or had I just humiliated myself and Sky for nothing?

"It was good humiliation," Sky pointed out when I commented. "Power's a good aphrodisiac."

"Remind me to become a politician sometime."

I liked the way she rolled her eyes. "Okay, *some* power is a good aphrodisiac."

"Has she done that kind of thing before?" I asked, curious.

"A few times. They weren't as good." She wrinkled her nose. "The problem with having male bits is I can't fake an orgasm to get out of it."

The barman came over and gave her a nod, and Sky stood. "Wait here, I'll be back in a sec."

I drank a gulp of my water and waited, trying to stay calm. Should I leave? I could just walk out, make a clean getaway…

Sky returned a few minutes later. "So, yours?"

I knew better than to ask; she obviously wanted to leave. "Sure."

She waited until we were walking along the street, and then said, "You impressed her. She didn't think you'd play."

I frowned. "But she…those were the demands. She didn't think I wanted the documents?"

"She would have settled for less. She wanted to see how far

you'd go."

I had a sinking feeling in my stomach. "Shit. So?"

Sky shrugged. "You passed. She'll give you what you want. You might get offered a job if something likely comes up."

"Why?"

I got another shrug. "The documents have already gone to the buyer. It doesn't matter if you get them now."

I let out a sigh. I'd paid too much for something that they didn't think was important. Bah. "Always the politics, huh?"

"That's the world. Anyway, your buyers won't care when they get them."

I eyed her. "Huh?"

"Well, they only need the proof. They're not acting on the information."

My stomach was dropping. My hands felt cold. My brain was in overdrive.

"You think I didn't look in to you?"

She'd found something. About me.

"He scotched one virus, sure. But he didn't find the other one."

Benny. Someone had hacked Benny's computer.

"And it was easy enough to put a tracker on your phone."

I finally managed to move, pulling my phone out of my pocket. She'd bugged it. I went to flip the back cover off, take the battery out, destroy the card, wipe the information—

Sky just shrugged. "It's done the work. Destroy it if you like."

I clenched it in my fist. "What do you know?"

"Nikolas Jinsen, third rank field de-tect-ive."

Shit. She knew.

I wanted to run.

No. It was a game.

She hadn't sold me out. I had walked out of there. I had to see this through.

I took a moment to get my anger and fear under control, and then looked down at her. "What do you want from me?"

Sky's bright eyes looked up at me. "She doesn't know."

That took a moment. "The Queen doesn't? You're *blackmailing* me?"

She shook her head. "Nah. Not my style."

"So, what?" If she wasn't going to threaten me with a reveal, what was the point of telling me?

"I want to help."

I managed to shut my mouth before I caught any flies. "You want to help? Help *me*? Why?"

"I'm bored." We'd stopped in the middle of the street, people hurrying past us, ignoring us. Sky pressed one finger into my chest. "I've worked for this lot for a few years, but I don't do much most of the time. You're more fun than I normally get. I want in."

"In me?"

"That too. I want..." And she gave me a wicked look. "I want you to use me."

I gave her a long look back, considering the proposal as my heartbeat slowed. Well, she knew the life, and it wasn't like I was averse to having a partner. I just needed to be wary of the little snake in my midst...

"And you'll use me?" I asked her.

"Absolutely." The look she gave me made my cock twitch against my jeans.

"You'll have to give me something."

"You know enough about me."

I considered. Well, I suppose I did. She was for hire, and she'd just told me her price. I slid my hand around the back of her neck, there in the crowded street, and pulled her against me. "I can't promise anything."

"You don't need to." Sky's lips were warm against mine, and I felt them move as I kissed her. "You'll pay my price."

"Yes, ma'am."

The blue-haired woman grinned up at me as we parted. "So. How about we discuss the details somewhere a little more private?"

I couldn't help the grin that crossed my lips. I liked this girl.

This was going to be fun.

***

"So," I said as we shut the door of my apartment. "What else do you know about me?"

She shrugged, eyes glinting. "You like getting into trouble, and getting out of it."

Despite myself, I laughed. "That's probably the best description I've come across." I gestured her through to my living room, which we hadn't made it to last time. The bedroom had got in the way.

Sky sat herself down cross-legged on my sofa and eyed me. "You act as the liaison. You carry dirty packages, hunt out the information, snitch on the vermin. You're an angel in a devil's world." She leaned back. "Why do you do it?"

"What, get into trouble?" I walked over to my tiny kitchen and pulled a can out of the fridge. "Drink?"

She considered, and then held out a hand. I tossed her the can and got another for myself.

"None of the usual reasons," I admitted, walking back around and sitting down on the chair opposite. I didn't want to be too close to her if this was the sort of conversation we were having. "I wasn't abused. Don't do drugs. Don't get in trouble…"

"A thirst for justice?"

I snorted and cracked the tab on the can. "I suppose so, but not for any particular reason. I guess I like puzzles. Adventures. And this is the best legal way I can skate on thin ice."

She was watching me, under that bright blue hair, her lean body somehow fitting into my sofa and my apartment and my life. "You like living on the edge, and you choose to do it on the side of the Angels."

"I'm a little bit devil," I agreed, taking a pull of the cold liquid. "It suits me."

She raised her eyebrows, and the mischievous look that she gave me made my cock stiffen in my jeans. "You are that."

"So how about you?" I asked. "How come you ended up working for her and stealing documents?"

"Walking out with them," she corrected. "I didn't steal them." And then she leaned back against the sofa cushions and gave me a long, challenging stare. "You tell me. Surely you did your research?"

I took another pull of the can to give myself time to think. I had done my research, but I also liked holding some trump cards. How much to tell her?

"Well, you're fairly recognisable with that hair," I pointed out.

She shrugged. "It makes a good disguise."

"That's fair." It had taken a good couple of hours for me to recognise her as the electrician's helper, and if she hadn't stood in exactly the right way, I doubt I would have made the connection...at least before I'd got to know her. I'd be able to spot her in a crowd, now, if only because my cock would notify me.

She was still watching me from under that bright blue hair, and I wondered why she'd chosen that particular shade. It certainly stood out. Well, like she said, that was the point.

I took another drink, and then said, "You're a thief, although you don't get caught, and you pick your fucks with care. You work for a few people and don't have any particular loyalty to one group. You don't squeal, but then you've never really been under pressure." No one on the Angels' team had ever had enough evidence to bring her in for questioning. I wondered if that was because she made sure she stayed on the edges, or if she really was good enough to not leave traces.

The woman on my sofa smiled, as if I'd done a good job. "Not bad, Nikolas."

I abruptly made up my mind, for better or for worse. I wanted to rattle her—and to let her know that she wasn't the only one who could get secrets out. "And I know you're into gambling."

She shrugged, but I could see the faint tension in the gesture, despite the smile that touched her lips. "A girl's got to have some vices."

"Not when it gets you in debt, she don't."

The smile left her lips.

"And not when it means you're paying it back to the people who control the Queen."

She was tensing, and her knuckles on the can were white.

"It's not much, in money terms. But it's not just money, is it?"

For the first time, her voice cracked out of the higher register. "How…" She swallowed, and returned to the Sky I knew. "How did you find that?"

I shrugged. "Contacts."

"Benny." Her lips thinned, and then a thought crossed her face and she began to relax. "He can hack *their* files?"

"Some of them."

"Ohhhhh." It was a breath of pleasure, of anticipation. I wanted to hear it as I slid my lips around her cock…but that could wait.

I filed that idea in the 'later' box, and said, "To return to the debt subject." I wanted to finish prodding that wound right now. "Aren't you going to get into trouble when they find you're hanging around with me?"

Her eyes flicked to the bulge in my jeans, and I mentally filled in, '*We don't do much hanging*'. But what she actually said was, "Not if you're doing some work for the Queen. And I can fuck who I like."

"What if they find out who I work for?"

She blew a breath out through her nose, and looked down at the can. "I think I'd figure that out when I came to it. It depends on how deep I am at the time."

"You'd throw me under the bus?"

The bright eyes looked up and fastened on me, almost angry. "No. I don't squeal. But if you were already there, I'd save myself. You're just a fuck buddy, and the Queen likes you. I don't know you're working with the legals."

"How did you find that out?"

She considered, for a moment, and I could see the calculations going on behind her eyes. How much to reveal to me?

"The buyers asked me," she said after a moment. "So I checked who they had hired. Sounded like you, so it was easy enough to bug your phone when I was here."

"About that…" I said, and pulled it out of my pocket. "How did you hack it?"

She leaned over and took it off me with one quick gesture, moving back before I could pull her head in for a kiss. And then—

The bitch swiped in.

She knew my code. I mean, I know it's not the most secure of methods, but…after one date? One fuck? Really?

"How?" I snapped.

Her eyes slid up to mine. "I watch, Nikolas." She threw the phone back, and when I turned it over, I saw a new app on the screen.

"You installed…"

"All legal. It's not hackable, so…I didn't hack it."

I angrily uninstalled the app and slapped the phone down on the table next to me. "I'm buying a new one."

She just raised an amused eyebrow. "You don't have a burner sim?"

I huffed out another breath. "Trying to teach me my job?"

"You obviously need lessons."

Was she trying to wind me up? I surged up off the chair

and icily removed the can from her hand, placing it on the table. "You seem to be forgetting who's in charge here."

She couldn't stand when I was so close to her, but she did grin up at me, completely unrepentant. "You aren't proving it."

I was rough and fast. I pinned her to the couch and fucked her hard enough to make the legs move, jolt by jolt across the floor as I thrust in to her ass, gripping her thighs, her legs spread out and her hands tight on the cushions. I wanted to make her moan, make her pant, and she writhed and gasped and wanted me to go faster, harder, fuck her, please, please—

Her hand was on her cock and I felt her come, felt the muscles grab my cock and pull me deeper in, and then I was gone, frustration and anger and lust all melting together and racing out of me as my body shook.

We had made a mess of the sofa, but as we collapsed together onto the fabric, I didn't care. I was sweaty and out of breath; every muscle hurt and my cock twitched with sensation, but…

But oh, she was so good.

"You can't solve every problem with sex," she told me as we shifted into slightly more comfortable positions, still sounding out of breath. Her t-shirt was sticking to her chest, slick with sweat, and I doubted that mine was any better.

"Why not?"

She considered that, and then shrugged. "It's not always convenient."

"You wanted to be on my side." I carefully removed the condom from my softening cock and knotted the top. I'd have to sort out the mess on the sofa some time later.

"Doesn't mean I can't teach you a thing or two."

I ran my hand through her hair and kissed her salted lips. "All right, a bargain. You teach me your tricks, and I'll teach you mine."

"Partners, then."

"Oh, no." My hand tightened in her hair. "You're mine. I'm going to use you for as long as I want."

A shiver ran through her body, and I felt her breath ease out onto my cheek. "Really."

"In any way I want."

"I don't do pain," she warned me. "Not majorly."

"I'll just spank you when I need to get something out of you," I told her, "and use you for my pleasure the rest of the time. Fair?"

"As long as I get to come too, that's fine."

"Then we've got a deal."

We sealed it with a kiss.

And then we went to work.

Chapter Four

My first step was to introduce Sky to Benny. He stopped playing Halo long enough to press the door entry button, and I led her up the three flights to his apartment.

They didn't get off to the best start. Benny did briefly tear his eyes away from his game when Sky was introduced, and then hesitated, paused the game, and turned.

He looked her up and down, and then looked at me. "*That* Sky?"

I nodded. "She's going to—"

"She's a man." Benny doesn't do subtle, or polite.

"I'm a woman," Sky said, managing a mild tone. "And I prefer female pronouns."

Benny gave her a long stare, and then nodded.

Sky held out a hand.

"Uh, Benny doesn't do touching," I butted in.

Sky's glare softened, but she left the hand out. "Fist bump?"

And Benny gave her a fist bump.

"So, what have you got for me?" I asked Benny.

"Why is she here?" Benny *really* isn't subtle.

"Nikolas offered me a better deal," Sky said, and then turned to me. "What are you actually after?"

"Information," I said flatly.

"Do the Angels want to take everyone in the Queen's gang out?"

I hesitated. I'd wanted the documents, sure, but then I'd also wanted to know who stole them. And now I'd gotten a lot more than I'd bargained for.

I had an in.

"Why are you in on this?" I asked her. "I know you're bored, but...taking down an underground criminal group?"

She shrugged. "I work for them because I have to. I don't have much loyalty...and I don't like them. They've fucked me enough times." I couldn't work out if she was talking metaphorically or physically. "I'll be on the side of the Angels for a little while. But I want to know what I can do to help you."

"Angels." A half-smile appeared on Benny's face. "Cute nickname. Not heard the authorities called that before." Then the smile disappeared and he was all business again. "I need access. I can't get past their security."

Sky chewed her bottom lip. I wanted to fuck her right then, but this was business. Pleasure later. "What'd that involve?" she asked.

"A file onto their system. USB or package. Even email." Benny was fiddling with his nails in the way he always did when he had to actually talk to someone real. "Once it's on the system, it's untraceable. I assume you want me to monitor things," he added to me.

I slowly nodded. "Yes. I'd need to talk to the bosses, but… we monitor it, get them what they need. You can't get onto the whole system, so if you could…"

Sky was waiting.

"Information," I said to her. "Get Benny the in he needs, and then we just stay low, do small jobs, find out what we can. I'll confirm with the bosses but I reckon moles is the best way to go."

She nodded and looked at Benny. "I can get us in if you tell me how to implant it."

Benny swung back to his computer. "Talk to the boss first," he said to me, but his screen was already filling with code.

I raised an eyebrow at Sky.

"You talk to people," she said to me, "and then you call me."

***

I went to see my bosses.

They're a stiff-necked, cautious, boring bunch. They thoroughly disapproved of me, and I disapproved of them. They considered me reckless, and I considered them too slow. But they had seen my potential, hired me and gave me a direction. I did all the dirty work, and they didn't ask questions. Some people might find it annoying, but that was the way I liked it.

What they didn't know wouldn't hurt them—and in this particular case, I was not about to tell them how I'd got an in for the Queen's business. I was also not about to tell them just how much sex I was getting.

I did feel rather smug about it, though.

So I sat in the white-painted, file-laden office and spun my boss a yarn about information, moles, caution and secrecy. She loved the word caution, but loved the idea of juicy information even more. If I could get Benny access, then they'd have a whole file system at their fingertips.

"Can you get anything else?" my boss asked, drumming her fingers on the table. There are some women that I'm not attracted to, and I thanked my lucky stars that Detective DeVoy was one of them. That could have really complicated my job.

"Like who?"

"The Mardos organisation?"

I swallowed. "Uh, I can try. We'd assumed the Queen, but..."

"If you can get Benny a mole in there, too, then do it."

I nodded. "So we've got the go-ahead?"

"I'll have to pass it up the chain." She fixed me with a stare. "I don't ask about methods, Jinsen, and you don't tell. If you're caught, we'll deny everything."

I grinned at her. "Who would have ever thought that someone like me would be working under someone like you?"

And she leaned back in her chair and smiled back at me. "Exactly."

She might have been a stiff-necked, cautious legal, but I did like my boss.

***

It was two days later when we got the official go-ahead. Monitoring was approved, and if Benny could get into the files…great. I glossed over my use of Sky; if they kept tabs on me then they'd find out, but they'd given me a lot of freedom before. I just hoped that it extended to fucking someone who could do some serious damage.

But then she could have already done it.

I mentally shrugged. She was dangerous…and so was my job. That was what made it all the more fun.

I texted Sky as soon as I got the message, and got her to meet me at my place. I wouldn't risk another jaunt to Benny's —not with her, at any rate, in case someone was tailing her— and if they knew where my place was then they'd know about us already. Plus, it meant there could be fun times in my future.

Ok, ok, I was thinking with my cock. Who wouldn't be?

Sky was entirely composed when I opened the door to her, but as soon as it shut behind me she wound her hands around my neck and kissed me. I returned it, pushing her up against the wall and enjoying the feel of her body against mine.

"Business or pleasure first?" she murmured to me as we broke apart a little.

"We're going to have to do pleasure," I managed, "because I can't think straight."

And that mischievous glint told me that she already had a plan. Within three seconds, I'd been pushed back against the opposite wall, my fly was down, and Sky's warm mouth was heading for my rock-hard cock.

"Condom!" I groaned, putting one hand on her forehead.

"Unless you've got a clean test sheet on hand."

She made an apologetic face and dug one out of her back pocket. The cool of it was a relief to my aching cock, and then her lips were warm and soft, and I was lost. At some point I slid down the wall, coming to rest in a tangled heap of limbs on the hard floor, Sky twisting around and never losing contact. There could have been a parcel of thugs coming through the door and I wouldn't have been able to stop them, too engrossed in the feelings that she was pulling out of me.

Somehow, she built me up and up and up, and every time I thought I was going to come, it was just another peak; my heart was racing and my chest hurt from sucking in a breath any time the tension let up, just for a moment, before the spiral took me higher and higher.

And I cried out as I came, my fingertips trying to dig into the wooden floor.

When I managed to focus again, Sky wasn't there. The condom was still on my cock, and as I took it off I heard noise from the kitchen.

She stuck her head around the doorway as I pushed myself up. "Drink?"

"Coffee," I said fervently.

She grinned at me. "I wore you out that badly?"

"Yes." I groaned, feeling everything ache as I stood up. "And believe me, I'll pay you back for it."

"I'll believe that when I see it."

"Ugh. You tease." I shook my muscles out and headed to the kitchen.

Sky was rummaging in my cupboards, and glanced over her shoulder as I came in. "Coffee…"

"There." I leaned over her, pushing her hips against the counter as I did so, and fished the bag from the shelf. She'd filled the kettle at least, so I flicked that on while I kept her pinned.

"You're hurting me," Sky complained.

"Tough."

She ground her ass back into my crotch, making my breath hiss. I was still sensitive. "Stop it," I told her, pouring coffee grounds into a pot.

"Or what?"

I put the bag down, pushed her chest down onto the counter-top, and slid my hand down her very nice ass. "Or I make you stop."

"You like it."

"I do." I kept her chest pinned with one hand, and slid the other around her waist to flick the button of her jeans. Her hands came down and helped me, and I felt the belt loosen as her cock slid out. "But that doesn't mean I'm not going to remind you that there are consequences."

I pushed her jeans down and burnished her smooth, tight ass with a stinging handprint. I heard the breath hiss through her teeth, but when I looked down she had one hand around her cock and her forehead against the cool surface of the counter.

A second slap.

"Why do you like this so much?" I asked, curious.

A third slap.

"It's a game…" she managed, and the fourth slap made her moan. "It's sensation. I hate it." A fifth slap. "And I love it."

I could see her hand working, and I dealt out the sixth and

seventh slaps in quick succession, not giving her time to recover. I'd only intended to do ten, but I didn't get that far. As my hand landed for eight, her body jerked and spasmed, and she left a trail of white down one of the cupboards as the counter-top misted with her groan of pleasure.

I left her there to recover as I found a cloth, and then she put herself away and did up her jeans as I cleared up the mess.

The kettle was still hot, so I made us both coffee. She took hers along with the lingering kiss that I gave her, and smiled at me.

"So," I said as we looked at each other over the curling steam, cheeks flushed and bodies sated for the moment. "Shall we get to work?"

Chapter Five

The building didn't look like anything special from the outside; a faceless office in amongst multiple other offices. There was a door with a buzzer, and a camera. A lobby inside with some stairs. Nothing unusual. But this was the centre that controlled several million in assets, ran one of the largest drug and trafficking operations in the area, and was most likely involved in some other...more dubious operations. My side didn't have a lot of proof, and they wanted some.

That's where I came in.

This had taken several visits to set up; two to the Queen, to persuade her to hire me for more than just fucking people —and, incidentally, to get a small Benny-provided file onto one of her servers—and one back to Benny for the tiny USB now nestling under my watch. Sky had obviously persuaded the Queen that I was clean, or at least, I hadn't been taken out back and shot, so I was assuming my cover story had stood up. It was actually a damn good cover story, because it involved fights, arrests, deportations, trafficking and the occasional count of public drunkenness. Even better, most of it was real. To get into this world, all I had to do was be my former self.

It was why the Angels liked me so much. And why they hated me.

Sky pushed the buzzer and said, "Sky, expected."

"Just one moment." After a long minute when our profiles were obviously being checked on the door cam, the buzzer went and the door clicked open.

We weren't stupid enough to say anything as we crossed the lobby and headed for the stairs. I was officially Sky's thug power on this trip, and unofficially learning the ropes. The Queen had eyed me and told me that I may as well learn to be useful. I'd smirked, but thankfully she hadn't wanted a repeat of my first visit.

And so now I was following a blue-haired woman into the rat's nest. Fun times.

I'm not sure what I had expected, but it wasn't the tall, busty woman who looked up at us from a comfy armchair in the room we were shown into. There were several huge screens on the wall across from her, a desk to her right with a sleek laptop on it, and a handful of besuited thugs standing around; so far, all business. But she had a small dog nestled in her lap, an expensive handbag by her exquisitely shod feet, and a stare that said she'd be happier not seeing us treading across the maroon carpet. This wasn't what I was expecting for the head of the Mardos.

"What?" she snapped.

"The Queen—" Sky started.

The woman put the dog down and stood. She was a good few inches taller than Sky in her heels, and she made a point of looking down her nose. "Yes, I got the message. I didn't realise she'd send *you*." She looked at me. It was a level stare, as she was almost exactly the same height as me. "And *this* is?"

I had to swallow before I managed to say, "Nikolas." I wondered at the possessive note in Sky's tone, and then, as the woman stepped forward, I realised that Sky had done me a favour. I was her fuck-toy…and that made me oh so desirable to this woman.

"Charmed. I'm Tanya." She ran her eyes down and then back up my body with a softer expression, but her eyes hardened as she turned back. "If you're just collecting, you can deal with someone else."

"No," Sky said, sounding irritated. "We need to discuss —"

And Tanya backhanded Sky across the face. "Quiet, freak."

My chest burned as I sucked in a breath. I wanted to defend her, to shout the woman down, to hit her in return. I wanted to tell Sky that she wasn't a freak.

But there were thugs around. And I had a job to do.

She'd attacked Sky.

No. Stay put. Don't start anything.

"She tolerates you, pervert," Tanya said as Sky stumbled back. I put out a hand and steadied her. "But I won't. He'll do for a messenger. Get out."

Sky ignored my hand on her back, and spat blood at Tanya Mardos' feet, invisible on the crimson carpet. And then she turned, and walked out.

I was on my own.

But she'd got me past the first stage.

***

Ten minutes later, I was in the lap of luxury. And this time, it hadn't been Sky who'd got me in. It was the dog.

I've always liked animals, and as soon as Sky left, the dog had jumped down from the seat and come to investigate. I bent down to say hello, and turned on my charm.

"You like dogs?" Tanya said as I fussed the happy little thing.

"He's a beautiful one. What breed is he?"

And it turned out that Tanya was more than ready to be charmed, particularly when it came to her little Petros. She swept me and the dog off through a heavy door into a private room, where a flunkie handed me a glass of wine and settled me on a very plush sofa. Petros bounded along by my feet, rolled over to be fussed, hopped up on the sofa beside me and generally adored the attention. When I caught a glimpse of Tanya's face, it was obvious that she wasn't going to completely let her guard down, but I'd certainly got myself in there.

"So you have dogs?" Tanya asked from her chair opposite.

"My apartment won't allow them," I said ruefully as Petros settled himself with his chin on my lap, more than happy to doze now he'd had some excitement. "I do miss them. I used to have two Dachshunds as a kid, and I dog-sat my neighbour's terrier. Small dogs are better, aren't they?"

"One of the few things that are." She smiled. "I usually prefer larger. So, you come with a recommendation from the

Queen?"

I blinked, rather astonished at the turn the conversation had taken. "I do?"

"Oh, yes." I was quite surprised that she wasn't a cat person. That had definitely been purred. "Apparently you were most obliging."

"You've done your research." I smirked at her.

"I always do. Are you exclusive with anyone?"

I briefly wondered what she'd do if I said Sky. Throw me out of her rooms, most likely, and probably disinfect everything I'd touched. But I had a tiny USB under my watch strap, and a job to do. I shook my head and petted the ears of the tiny dog on my lap. "I'm always up for a good time, ma'am." I glanced down. "Although I'm afraid that right now I am taken…"

She laughed. "You are a man of priorities. Business first, and then…pleasure?"

"Of course, ma'am."

***

I got what the Queen wanted—Tanya negotiated hard, but then so did I. I managed to keep her sweet, and we settled on only a little less than what I'd been officially told to get. Of course, unofficially, I'd been given other figures, and I'd more than topped those. A definite win for the man with the cute dog snoring on his lap.

Tanya ordered a refill of drinks once we'd reached an agreement, and Petros apparently decided that was more interesting now he'd had his nap. As he moved, Tanya did too. "Wait," she ordered me, and swept out.

She'd left a slim laptop on the small desk at the side of the room, and I hesitated. Should I make the most of the opportunity?

But something itched at my nerves. This felt like a trap.

I wandered over to the window instead, and used the reflection to work out where the cameras would be. She had to have some in here, particularly as there was a laptop oh-so-free for the spying on. Yeah, there were two glints, and I'd bet that the mirror held a general one.

Call me paranoid, but I'm usually right.

I opted to admire her view, which was looking down into the plaza below, and drink my very good Prosecco. When Tanya swept back in, I caught approval in her gaze. "You like my view?"

"Very much." I was enjoying people-watching, and camera-spotting.

"Come and see my other one."

I should have just done it when she'd left the room, I thought. And then got myself kicked out, probably with broken legs.

I was here for a job. She was inviting me in. I'd got some measure of trust.

She'd hurt Sky.

I'd get another opportunity. I had to go through with this.

I gave Tanya Mardos a charming smile, and followed her through the doorway.

***

Her bedroom was as large as the room we'd just left. It contained an enormous bed, two doorways—one of which I guessed was a bathroom, and the other was open a crack to reveal clothing strewn across the floor—and a wall made entirely of windows looking out onto the city beyond.

Tanya shut the door behind me and put her glass on the wide desk that sat in the centre of the room. My eyes fastened on the slim laptop that lay on this desk, too. Did that woman have a laptop for every room?

And then my attention was dragged elsewhere. Tanya was stepping out of her dress.

I didn't gape; I'm not that much of a teenager. But it did capture most of my attention. She undressed like it was a show, and so I stood and admired. The dress slid down, revealing a larger bust than I'd suspected, and slips of silk and lace for underwear. Those came off next, leaving her with just her heels. She stepped out of those, and then…

She walked over to the window—the completely clear, floor-to-ceiling, plate glass window—and pushed herself against it.

And she turned her head to me, and said, "Fuck me here."

Oh, crap.

Well, I should have expected it. But there are some days when my job really isn't worth it.

I took a large gulp of my drink and then placed the glass down on the desk. My watch went next to it. And then I stepped out of my jeans, pulled my t-shirt over my head, and walked naked over towards her.

The windows covered the entire side of the room, and as I reached the edge behind Tanya, I felt incredibly exposed. We were however-many flights up and I could see the people walking down below, apparently oblivious to the naked woman spreadeagled above them. There were buildings around, with windows; some were on the same level, and while

I couldn't quite see inside them, we were very visible here. Tanya was on display for the world.

Her breasts were pushed against the cold surface, curving up, and as I ran my fingers down her spine she slid her gloriously rounded ass back against me. Even though I felt like the world was watching, I couldn't resist.

But I'd give her, and the world, a tease.

I sank to my knees behind her and then turned, ducking between her legs, and buried my face in her cunt. She loved it. She spread her legs for me, her breasts still pressed against the glass, and I felt the cold of it against my back as she thrust against my tongue. I was leaning out against nothing, feeling as if I would just tip over into the shards of the window if it broke and fall all the way to the square below...

Tanya moaned above me, throwing her head back, writhing against the glass. I wondered if anyone was watching as I flicked with my tongue and she threw her hands above her head, lifting her breasts, thrusting herself harder against my mouth. She was putting on quite a show.

She came just as dramatically, screaming out her pleasure as her palms left long streaks down the glass.

As she pushed herself away from the window and from me, it didn't look faked; she was sweaty and glowing, her eyes lit with a lustful hunger. Well, I couldn't judge—exhibition wasn't my bag but it was obviously hers, if the smears on the windows were anything to go by.

She walked over to the table to pick up her abandoned glass, and handed mine to me as I joined her. "You like my cinema?"

"How many people do notice?"

She smiled. "No one. It's one-way glass. But I love the feeling; so many tiny people, and I am on display for all of them."

"Now that is smart," I said, draining the glass. She didn't taste bad, but let's face it, I'd rather that cunts tasted of Prosecco.

"You can fuck me there too, in a moment. Let me just check my business."

"Yes, ma'am."

As she opened the door, Petros ran in. She ignored him and left, and as he ran under her desk and the tiny frisson of fear slid down my spine, I went for it.

Under the guise of rescuing my glass and scooping up Petros, I retrieved the tiny USB and slid it into the side port of her laptop. If someone slowed down the camera that was likely in here then they'd catch me, but hopefully they wouldn't bother. After all, I hadn't fiddled with the laptop in the other room when I had the opportunity…

And then I took the dog out into the main room, where Tanya—still completely naked—was talking to a man with a slight paunch and carefully combed hair. As I approached, I saw his eyes scan me; and then he raised an appreciative eyebrow, took the dog with a nod of thanks, and turned back to Tanya. I took my dismissal with good grace, and retreated back to the bedroom. If I could get my clothes and grab the USB on my way out…

Tanya came back in a few minutes later, just as I was exiting the bathroom from a much-needed piss. "Now, we fuck."

Well, I was still on the job.

So I pushed her against the sheet of glass, and I fucked her until she moaned and screamed and writhed. It should have been glorious; I hadn't fucked a woman in a while, and I'd forgotten how warm and wet cunts are, how rounded asses and firm thighs make for so much sensation.

But the echo of the slap was still ringing in my brain. And so I pinned the woman to the window and thrust harder and harder, digging my fingers into her rounded hips, pressing her breasts against the cold glass and slamming myself into her. I fucked her as hard as I could, trying to get even a little, tiny piece of revenge on the woman who'd hurt—

She came, screaming out her pleasure, and I gave her one final, savage thrust before I withdrew. I wasn't close. I couldn't be. Not with that bitter taste in my mouth.

We'd left more smears on the glass, and Tanya smiled approvingly at them as we straightened up. "You can shower in there," she told me, pointing at the bathroom. "I will finish myself again."

I raised my eyebrows. "You have quite a sex drive."

"I put my business first," she told me, "and so when I take pleasure, I like to take it all at once. But I find men can rarely keep up."

She headed for the desk and her laptop, and I was obviously dismissed. I scooped up my clothes, retreated to the bathroom and made the most of the gloriously large, hot shower to try to recover some composure. Would Benny's program work? Would it be the right laptop? He'd said that he only needed a minute, and then I could take the USB out. I hoped that he was right.

I dried myself on the smallest towel I've ever encountered,

and wondered if it was deliberate. It would certainly show flesh. And then I dressed, smoothed back my hair, and headed back out into the room.

Tanya was sitting in front of her open laptop, her legs spread and her hands moving between her thighs. I tried not to show the surge of relief. So, could I get the USB out?

I walked around behind Tanya and ran my hand up her body, tweaking her nipples. She was watching porn, but moaned as my hands grazed over her. "Yes. Yes."

I stepped over her outstretched leg and pushed the laptop out of the way, turning the porn soundtrack down and neatly palming the USB drive as I did so. As I turned back, she was watching me, bright-eyed.

"You don't need accompaniment," I said, planting my ass on the desk where the laptop had been. "You're hot enough. I want to see you finish."

Her eyes brightened, and she spread her legs further. "You want to watch me?"

"Come for me."

And she did; one hand playing with her nipple, the other at her cunt, her head tipped back and her body writhing in the chair. She was hot, I had to admit—but not quite as hot as Sky, moaning beneath me, her hips bucking against mine. But I kept that thought to myself.

As Tanya finished, panting, I slid off the desk and leaned forward to kiss her wet, open mouth. "I'll see myself out."

She caught my chin as I started to straighten. "You leave your number at the desk. I like you."

"Yes, ma'am." I'd done it. I grinned at her, and strolled out.

***

The man and Petros were waiting for me in the other room, and I gave the man a charming smile as Petros bounded over for more fusses. "I have to leave my number. Are you the best person to leave it with?"

"Of course." He was eyeing me again, taking in my wet hair. I wondered if he'd appreciate the chance to have my number, too. That could be a useful in. Was everyone in this damn organisation as horny as hell?

I left my number on the back of a spare business card, gave the man another smile, gave Petros a quick fuss, and then strolled out.

Not bad at all, I thought. Not bad.

Sky wasn't waiting, but then I suspected she hadn't wanted to wait with the eyes of the Mardos on her—and with a livid handprint on one cheek. I stopped briefly in the square, dropping the tiny USB down a handy drain as I looked up at the floors and tried to guess which window was Tanya's. She was right, they were one-way; from here they were mostly darkened, and I couldn't see anything beyond the mirrored finish.

And then someone lightly touched my arm. "Nikolas?"

I turned. It was a man, small and compact, with a shaved head and a quick smile. "I have a gun under my coat. Please come with me."

I caught the flash of movement and the brief glimpse of barrel, and the moment crystallised around me as instinct took over. I could run, fight. It'd be relatively simple...

"We simply want to talk to you," the man said, still smiling. "The gun is to ensure you know we are serious."

He only came up to my shoulder, but the gun did make a difference. I'd been shot before. It hadn't been fun. "I prefer chocolates," I said.

"I will bear that in mind for next time."

Oddly, that was reassuring; they did intend for there to be a next time. Well, I'd have to go with it. I spread my hands and smiled back. "So?"

"There is a car waiting."

We strolled across the square. Maybe I should have run, but I didn't doubt that he would have shot me. It's something in the eyes, and this man…I'd seen his type before. He was a man for hire, and he'd get the job done.

And weirdly, I liked him. We understood each other.

"Can I know your name?" I asked him.

"Jim." He gave me another smile. "I'm the odd-job man."

I think he liked me, too. But he opened the rear door of a car, and got into the passenger seat once I'd got in the back. There was a screen between myself and the front, and I heard the locks click as the car pulled away.

Well, all I could do was relax and watch the city…go… past…

Chapter Six

There was a white ceiling above me. One of those damn contoured ones that looked like it had been done by a duck, with the paintbrush held in its beak.

I blinked.

The last thing I remembered was the car.

And now I was lying on something soft, and the damn ceiling was doing circles above me.

Bloody hell, I was tired.

I managed to turn my head. It was a pretty generic hotel room, from what I could figure out. A pair of cheap curtains. A wide bed. A table and TV. White walls. The sort of corporate stuff they buy in bulk and throw at travellers.

It didn't give me any clues about how the hell I'd gotten here, though.

My head felt really muzzy, and my eyes were tired. I

couldn't think straight. That damn ceiling was wavering, going around and around in circles. If I found that duck, I'd eat it with mint sauce.

No, wait. That was lamb. What did you eat with duck?

For some reason, that really concerned me.

I heard the door click, and rolled my head. It was the small man. Jim. And a woman behind him, with brown hair and glasses.

"Nikolas," the woman said. "How are you feeling?"

"What do you eat with duck?" I asked her. My voice was sort of slurred, but I really needed to know.

She frowned at me. "Is this some sort of joke?"

"Plum sauce," Jim filled in from behind her.

"Yes!" I told him. "That's it! You're the bestest dude. You got it!"

I saw his mouth twitch. He thought it was funny too, and I cracked up laughing. The ceiling was whirling again and there were voices somewhere in the room, but I knew what I'd eat the duck with, so it didn't bother me. Plum! Plum. That's what you eat duck with…

***

When I opened my eyes again, there was a woman sitting next to me. Jim was there, too, sitting on a chair. The woman was blonde. Long legs. Tight clothes. I wasn't sure why she was there.

She curled her long legs up onto the bed and started stroking my chest. "Nikolas…"

"No," I said, annoyed, and tried to get my hands to move to push her away. I was so tired, and all I managed was some kind of weird flapping motion. "No."

"You have a girlfriend?" the blonde said, pouting. But she did stop stroking me.

"I work with this girl." I didn't want to tell her, but words were spilling out of me. My head rolled back against the pillows. "She's not a girl. But she is." I wasn't meant to say that. She didn't want me telling.

"Sky," someone murmured in the background. "One of the Queen's people. Blue hair."

"Does she have blue hair?" the blonde asked.

"Oh, yeah." The memory of my hands in it was turning me on. "Yeah."

"So what work do you do?" the blonde asked me.

"It's really hard work." I could feel my cock pulsing in my jeans. "Hard work." I giggled. I'd made a pun. No, wait. A pun was...I didn't know. Something else.

I drifted in and out of reality. I know there were other questions, but I was Nikolas, lying on a bed. Where did I live...did it matter? Stealing things? Sky had stolen me. Fucked me. Police...no, I hadn't slept with them. I didn't like sleeping with the police. They didn't relax.

"One-track mind," someone muttered.

What had I done with Tanya? I told them, in detail. And what did I do for the Queen? I told them that, too. Did I know anything about their business dealings? I laughed at that. I'd had hot sex. I didn't know about business. I didn't care.

The room was circling round me.

"Do you often work for the Queen?"

"Only when she wants me to." The blonde leaned over me, looking interested, and I told her conspiratorially, "She likes to watch."

"This still isn't getting anywhere," a female voice said from behind the blonde. "We gave him too much. He won't even feel pain in this state. We'll try again tomorrow."

The blonde got off the bed, but I didn't mind. She didn't have blue hair.

I laughed. It seemed like the funniest thing in the world. "I like her. I really like her," I said to the air. I was so tired. "I really, really..."

***

When I woke the next day I was lying on a bed, still fully clothed, and the sunlight was streaming in through the curtains. My head felt like a cat had slept in it, and it had definitely gone to the toilet in my mouth. I was thirsty, tired, and everything ached.

Drugs. I wondered what they'd used. What I'd said.

Well, nothing ached, and I was still clothed, so...

I remembered the blonde, and the voice, and I shivered. That had been too close.

I shoved myself off the bed and went to the loo, then found a drink. The door was locked, but I'd deal with that in a moment. I washed my face, tried to get rid of some of the headache, and had a look out of the window. I was on the fifth floor of what looked like a generic hotel—I could see rooftops some way below. If I jumped, I'd likely break something—and the window was one of the ones that only opened a little for air. I could break it...

There was a knock on the door, and then it opened. It was a slim, dapper man with dark hair. He eyed me standing by the window, and we faced each other in silence for a moment.

I could take him. I could make a break for it...

He jerked his head. "Follow me."

My heart jumped in my chest, but I kept my face steady.

I'd follow. Oh yes, I'd follow.

We walked in silence down the steps, and down past reception. Sky nodded to the receptionist and slid a key across the desk. I didn't want to ask what lies she'd spun to get it in the first place.

And then we were out onto the streets. Sky hailed a cab, we got in, and headed into the city traffic.

"Benny hacked their feed," Sky said without preamble.

"They recorded me?" That made me go cold. "Did I say anything…?"

Sky shook her head, but gave me a sideways glance, a smile creeping across her face. "You had a very one-track mind. You wouldn't shut up about a blue-haired girl you were sleeping with."

Her hand caught me a stinging blow across the face. I landed against the door, my head ringing.

And then she was kissing me. It was bloody uncomfortable, wedged between the door and the seat with my jaw stinging, but I wasn't about to complain.

When she finally released me, I shoved myself upright. "What the hell was that for?"

"You got caught, and you didn't say anything stupid."

"He had a gun." And then my brain caught up. "Wait, I didn't say anything stupid? I told them about you!"

Sky just gave me a smile that quite clearly said 'You idiot'.

"You don't mind them knowing?"

"They know already. You were so fixated on sex that you didn't tell them anything else."

That sank in, and I slumped back in the seat. "Oh god." I rubbed my face, and tried to focus. "Um. Yeah. So why did you spring me? Assuming you are springing me?"

"Yeah, we're going back to yours. They weren't getting anything good out of you last night, so they were going to try again today. I figured you'd rather that didn't happen."

I glanced out of the cab window at the rain, and nodded. "Thanks."

She smiled, looking out at the damp city, and her hand touched mine. We sat in silence for the rest of the journey, fingers locked together, each with our own thoughts.

***

She paid the cab off a street before my door, and we walked the rest of the way in the morning light. I spent a chunk of it admiring the dapper man next to me. She'd tied her hair back, and dyed it black. The suit was cut to fit, and looked good. She even walked differently.

"So who were they?" I asked as we got to my door.

"We call them the Jacks. I guess they noticed you working for the others and wanted to know more." Sky stuck her hands in her pockets as I got my keys in the lock, as casual as could be. "You're intact, at least."

"Yeah. Thanks to you. Did Benny get everything?"

She grinned as we got inside. "Yep. He's in, and he doesn't think they've noticed. You did good."

I felt the tension leave me. Tanya had paid off, despite the price. "Um, Sky...thanks for getting me in there."

Her mouth was faintly swollen, but it was barely noticeable. She rolled her eyes at me. "Just don't make me do it too often. I don't like them."

"It shows." She was walking ahead of me to the kitchen, and I got to admire her. "You know, you make a good man," I said to her.

"Thanks," she said dryly, not turning.

"Sky..."

She turned back, her face tight.

"That was the wrong thing to say?" I didn't touch her, even though I wanted to. Her tight posture said she wouldn't appreciate it. "You seem ok with your cock. You're really confident about your body."

"I'm a woman," Sky said, with a tension in her that I hadn't seen before. "I'm confident with sex, but I don't really feel comfortable dressing as a man."

I didn't entirely get that, but it was obviously a sore subject, and so I went to sit on the sofa as she went into the kitchen. She brought me over a can of drink without asking, and cracked her own open as she sat down on the edge of the chair. I let the silence hang, knowing she wanted to say more, but was just trying to find the words.

"I'm saving up for surgery," she said after a moment, low-voiced, looking at her can. It was odd to see a dark-haired man in Sky's place. But I could see her familiar mannerisms underneath the mask. "That's why...that's why I was gambling. Trying to get the money. I do win, often, but it's slow."

"But you have a debt to them..."

She made a sound, a faint huff of breath, and I stopped.

"They don't understand," she said eventually. "The Queen does. She's been helping. But they...see it as something to hold over me. Tanya kept sending me women, trying to convert me back. You…" And she lifted her head and smiled at me. "You saw me as me."

I found myself smiling back. "What can I say? My cock likes what it sees." Then I sobered. "You want surgery?"

"When I've got the money. I don't like this meat," and she gestured at her crotch. "Even though it feels good. I don't want huge breasts, or…or anything big changed. I just want my body to reflect the person I am."

I nodded. I could understand that, even if I was happy in my own body. "How much?"

She tried to shrug it off, but I could see the tension still in her eyes. "More than I've saved."

I wasn't exactly Mister Money, and so I filed it all away for later consideration. "You'll get there. So, you want to get out of that suit?"

She relaxed a bit. "I thought you'd never ask."

"What about your hair?"

"It's washable."

"Shower time." I grinned at her. "Let's wash it all away…"

The pained groan I got was definitely worth the bad joke.

***

I only had a small shower, and while I routinely swore at it when I bashed my elbows every morning, for Sky and myself? It was perfect.

Two bodies, pushed closed together under the spray. I soaped her hair and chased the waves of black that ran down her body, painting me in stripes as they went until Sky's hands wiped my skin clean in turn. I had to be close to her, had to kiss her open mouth, had to run my hands through her hair and down her back, pulling her against me. The soap turned our skin into silk and we glided across each other.

Water isn't the best lube—seriously, don't try it—and soap suds hurt, so we just turned each other on until it was painful and then tumbled out of the steamy compartment and into the bedroom, dressed only in towels that didn't catch all of the water.

We had time, and so I was gentle. I kissed up her legs, across her stomach, circled her nipples with my tongue until she writhed under me. Her hands clutched at my back and shoulders as I ran my lips up her neck and into the faint graze of rough stubble that she hadn't got round to shaving. Her damp hair curled round my fingers as I kissed her lips, her cheeks, her forehead, and then went back down to her ankles and did it all again.

When I did push my cock into her it was with a slow, easy grace. We gently moved together, skin on skin and mouth against mouth, her hands playing with my hair and my fingers curving around her buttocks, rocking back and forth. My climax was almost unbearable, sweet and long, and when I came back I had my head on her shoulder, my lips pressed against her skin as if trying to push my moans inside her with my pleasure.

I turned her onto her back and finished her with my lips, flicking the tip of her cock, playing with my tongue, sucking to draw out the orgasm and swallowing down everything she gave me. When she'd finished, I felt her wriggle down the bed and then she curled up into me in the mess of sheets and blanket, her damp hair against my shoulder and her legs twined into mine; and we slept.

***

I woke to a mug of coffee, as dark as a moonless night, and Sky sitting half-dressed on the floor, drinking her own mug. The black dye had dulled her hair, and now she was a beautiful cloud-grey, making me think of rain. It muted her skin, and made her more pensive than the vibrant woman I'd met…how long ago? It seemed like weeks.

I sat on the edge of the bed and drank my coffee, feeling the darkness roll into my veins like a tide. It was blissful.

I agreed to dinner with Sky, groped her ass as she left to run errands, got another shower, and then headed off to find lunch and run my own errands. I did have to stop by my bosses and see if they were happy, but beyond that, I had people to see, places to be, things to do.

Well, one person to do.

That thought made me stop cold in the street. Fuck, she really had spoiled me.

And then I started walking again with a smile crossing my lips. I didn't mind.

Hell, I didn't mind one single fucking bit.

Chapter Seven

S ky was already waiting in the bar when I got there that evening; the same bar that I'd first met her in, accompanied by her boring blonde friend. She hadn't yet dyed her hair back, but I thought that the grey suited her. It was more subtle, sure, but it made her look more professional.

She snorted when I told her. "I've got an appointment tomorrow. Don't get too used to it."

"I could buy you glasses. You could be a sexy librarian."

That got another snort. "All the librarians I know are more likely to kill you for not returning a book than fuck you."

"Stop spoiling my fantasies," I said, but my attempt at petulance was spoiled by my smile.

She gave me a look that I couldn't decipher. "If you like it that much, I'd consider keeping it."

I eyed her for a long moment, and then felt a rueful smile

cross my own lips. "Sky, I'd take you however you look. I like it, but I like you with blue hair too. Do whatever makes you feel comfortable." I leaned back. "Although I am a sucker for heels."

She rolled her eyes. "Have you got any idea how hard it is to find heels in my size?"

"Just sayin'."

We ordered food and sat at a small table in the corner, surrounded by chatter. "So," I said after we'd got most of the way through our food. "My bosses are happy. And I've got a proposition for you."

Her eyes lit up, and that mischievous smile I so liked touched her mouth. "Oh, really?"

"Not that kind of proposition."

"Damn."

"The Angels want to pay you to be a mole."

She sobered immediately. "What?"

"A year on their payroll. They want a long-term sting for information, and they're willing to pay you."

"How much?"

I named the figure, and saw her eyes go vacant. I let her work it out, and saw the brightness as she realised how much it was. "Would that be enough?" I asked quietly.

She nodded.

I tried to think of a good way to say it, but ended up with, "You gotta stop gambling, though. You'll never save enough if you do that."

Unexpectedly she grinned at me, and a strange warmth kindled in my stomach. "What?" I asked her.

"I don't need to."

"What?"

She was still grinning at me. "You're enough of a risk, Nikolas. You're a thrill. I like that."

The warm feeling in my stomach wasn't just the food. It snaked through my chest, and I found myself smiling back at the woman opposite me. "Oh, really?"

She just raised her eyebrows at me. "A year…I can probably do a year."

"Maybe we should find somewhere more private to discuss the details."

And I got that beautiful, wonderful, delicious smirk, accompanied by bright eyes. "The devil's in the details."

"That I am."

BOOK TWO

IN BED WITH THE ENEMY

Chapter One

Of all the things I expected to hear as I stood in front of my boss' desk, it wasn't the phrase that came from her lips.

"Your girlfriend," she said deliberately.

Sky. Bright blue hair, a sarcastic way of talking, a wicked smile, and—incidentally, of course—excellent in bed.

"...yes?" I prompted after a moment of silence.

"You're getting too involved, Jinsen."

"She's been my ticket in to the gangs," I pointed out. "I can't exactly not be involved."

"You know what I mean."

I admit I did glare. "I get it. I'd also like to hear your suggestions for other options, considering how successful I've been in getting you information."

My boss sighed and looked down at the sheet of paper in

front of her. "Yes, I'm aware of that. It's the only reason you're not on suspension."

My stomach dropped. I really was in the shit.

"I'm not sure how, but the higher levels have become aware of your girlfriend...and the position she occupies in the organisations we're currently investigating."

Fuck. Fuck, fuck, fuck.

Sky wasn't exactly important, for sure. She was more a runner, an information-collector, a...well, a thief. But she knew everyone, and even though our first meeting had been mostly accidental, I'd made sure I kept in her good books once I found out what she could do for me. The fact that the sex was fantastic and we actually got on really well was just a huge bonus.

But if the Angels had twigged that I was hooking up with someone who might not be strictly good for me...

My boss was talking. "...know you're not exactly bound by the same regulations normal Detectives are, Jinsen, so I'm happy to give you some leeway. You've provided some excellent sources of information over the last six months."

I waited for the 'but'.

"But I can't overlook this if my bosses are aware of it. You have to distance yourself from her, Jinsen."

I'd gone through the fear stage, and I was now into anger. "You dragged me in to give me another urgent assignment, and then you tell me to dump my information source, right? How do you expect me to get into the Jacks without being able to use the resources that got me in to the first two? You're gonna look bad as well when I can't come up with the goods."

"You'll find a way." My boss is more than capable of

standing up to me, which I hate. Life would be a lot easier if everyone just did things my way. "Dump the girl, Jinsen. They're going to be watching you."

"Am I on probation?" I knew I sounded sulky.

"Not yet."

I slammed the door on my way out.

***

So, now I had a whole list of problems.

The assignment I'd been called in for was actually fairly interesting. Over the last six months, Sky, my tech friend Benny and I had wormed our way into the good books—and data—of two of the criminal gangs in the city. They provided most of the girls, giggles and illicit substances that floated around—not to mention the illegal cash transactions, rip-off bargains and general good times that go with having a bunch of people around who see the law as flexible and people as a commodity. We'd gained a good amount of intel, and the police were having the time of their little lives planning raids.

Now, the Angels wanted in on a third organisation: the Jacks. I'd had them on my radar for a while—since they kidnapped me, actually—but I'd been too busy to really do much work. The Angels had obviously decided that this was the point they needed information, and for whatever stupid operational reasons, they wanted it fast. So they'd handed it to me. Without any details, of course—just a hand-wave and "get this done, quick" attitude. Fuckers. But I guess that's what I get for being too useful.

Problem number one was that honestly, I was too fuckin' busy to take on another organisation. I'd wormed my way into the Queen's good books by acting as a courier, busy-body and general runner, and between myself and my girlfriend Sky, we'd been bouncing around the city for the last six months. It had been a great way to get information and talk to absolutely everyone—and had got me some excellent leads, witnesses and information—but if I now had to somehow get into the Jacks…

That was problem two—actually getting my way into the Jacks. In six months, I had only met three of them, and only managed to get close to one. This wasn't something I could do in my spare time.

And problem three…dump Sky, or get the Angels peering over my shoulder.

My stomach clenched at the thought. Between the Devil and the deep blue sea, that's my life.

***

I admit that it wasn't just the contacts that made Sky so interesting to me. She'd hooked me fair and square the first time we met, and while she had got me into some very interesting places, she'd also got me into some very interesting positions.

In short, the sex was great, and I was not about to give that up because the big boss had decided that if he didn't get a fuck, I didn't either.

Screw that.

But that didn't mean I could ignore the ultimatum. I liked the paycheck, and…well, the Angels were one of the few organisations that I was happy in. I'd already dug myself out of the gutter once, and while I definitely wasn't of the right mentality to be a full-time police paper-pusher, I didn't want to go back into the gangs, either. So, to be able to live on the edge, get some danger, get some results…that's a good line for me, even if it was going to get me into trouble some day.

Well, it already had. Sky was definitely on the dishonest side of the grey line, but apparently she was now a step too far.

What to do? If I didn't at least look like I was obeying, they'd find out, and then bang goes my paycheck and my position and any chance of getting Sky out of her mess in a legal fashion. So, I had to get myself—nominally—out of the Queen's clutches and into the Jacks. All without screwing Sky.

I sighed, deciding that I needed a second opinion, and pulled out my phone to text Sky. And then I paused. How to tell her I had to dump her?

I decided to postpone that conversation. I'd focus on the Jacks; and that meant getting more information.

I went to see the Queen.

Chapter Two

T he Jacks?" the woman in front of me asked, and gave me a long look. I just looked back. "Why do you want to know?"

"Something Sky said," I said slowly. "I've been hanging out with Jim for almost six months, and I don't really know anything about him. I know he works for them, but he's remarkably closed-mouthed, and...I wondered if I should be worried. They did pick me up when I first started here..."

A pause, and then a nod. "You don't think it's suspicious that they haven't tried again?"

I shrugged. "I figured that as they'd seen me around more, working for you...you'd scared them off."

The Queen nodded. "Don't put all your eggs in that basket, Nikolas."

"Yes, ma'am."

"Well, you know a lot of what they do. Jack of all trades…safecrackers, hackers, security. They're specialists."

"Jim's good with a gun."

"Ex-forces, I believe."

I wondered what she knew about me. I wasn't good with guns.

"What do they want?"

"They're for hire." She seemed surprised that I didn't know that. "They usually want payment in information, though. Or skills. Help. Very rarely money."

"If they're hackers, I suspect they can get more than enough of that." Benny's lines of code somehow always kept him supplied with food and rent.

"There's a chapter here…about six of them, but I don't know the full extent of their contacts." The Queen snorted. "Just like they don't know mine. They stay out of my way, anyway. I don't like them, even if I have to use them."

"Have you got any contacts with them that would get me in to find out more?"

"Jim's your best one." That didn't answer the question, but looking at her face, I suspected that might be because she was trying to help. What were the rest of the Jacks like if Jim was the most likely chink in the armour? "Why are you suddenly interested?"

I gave a rueful smile. "My own fault, losing track of a threat."

I saw her eyes assessing me again. "You need protection?"

"No." I stifled a glare. I didn't want to offend her. "Seriously. I'm just…wondering why Jim's still hanging around me." And I was, now. The small, dapper man wasn't a natural friend for my lanky body and sarcastic personality—especially as he wasn't too keen on Sky, either. Why was he still meeting me for drinks? The Jacks hadn't been interested in me after that first attempt to get information—had they?

"Well, let me know. Can you take an assignment tomorrow?" the Queen added briskly.

Well, no time like the present to break bad news, but I had to find an explanation. I could tell her everything, sure, and then I'd likely get my kneecaps broken: telling a mafia boss whose information you're tapping that you're working for the Angels isn't likely to go down well. She didn't know about that—my kneecaps were intact—and I wanted to keep it that way. But if I lied, I'd have to back it up, and stick to it.

So I went for something in between. "Look, about that. Something's come up. I'm not going to have as much time for couriering for you."

Her eyes fastened on me, and then I got a rather judging look. "How long for?"

"I don't know yet."

There was a long moment of silence, and I felt myself start sweating. But I held on. She wanted me to break. She wanted me to talk. And I wasn't going to.

"We've got a big job coming up," the Queen said eventually. "You helped plan."

"It's not about that." I knew what she was asking. "I haven't sold you out."

"You been leaned on?" She was connecting dots.

"Not by them, or the Jacks. It's not connected to that."

The Queen left me in silence for another long moment, and then nodded. "You know that I value your services. I can probably find something else, but give me a day or two or work it out." The Queen's stare was still fixed on me. "Anything else you need to tell me?"

I gave her my best smile. "No. It's fixable, I just...need some time to fix it." That seemed like the best explanation. She nodded, and I got up.

"Nikolas..."

I turned back. The Queen was sitting at her desk, with an expression I didn't recognise on her face. Was that a hint of worry?

"Is it Sky?"

I tried to ignore the bolt of guilt that ran through my stomach. "No. No, we're good. I mean, I need to talk to her, but...we're good."

The woman's thoughtful eyes stayed on me as I left.

***

I had an immediate errand to run, and so I did that, jogging my way across town and trying not to think too much. I dropped off the parcel, got it signed for, picked up the information I needed, and then headed back towards the edge of the district and the Queen. My next assignment was with my flat and a quick shower, and then I had another appointment.

I started worrying about my problems again as I stepped out of my flat. Sky hadn't been there, which meant one conversation gratefully delayed. I decided that I'd sort of solved one problem, though: if I had managed to get the Queen off my back, then that was good. The Queen and Tanya Mardos were my two biggest clients, but I was peripherally involved in quite a lot of other things...mostly due to Sky. How was I going to explain any vanishing from that?

I was worrying over that as I headed downtown, until I caught something; a flash in a window that made me focus. Someone approaching from behind me. Someone trying to catch me up.

I gave them two streets, always staying a little ahead of them. Whoever it was, they were definitely following me, and not doing too good a job of it either.

The Angels? No. As far as they were concerned, I was doing what they wanted. They'd given their orders and I was jumping. Someone else? That possibility was more worrying. There were several people who would love a little chat with me, and I didn't really want a repeat of the last chat I had, which involved being drugged. Luckily I'd been too stoned—and too horny—to make much sense, but that didn't mean I'd get lucky again…

I did a quick calculation and decided that on a street, in public, was the best place to face whoever it was. If I ducked down a back alley and they were better than me, then I'd get beat. At least here someone might point and laugh.

I'm cynical, ok?

And so I slowed down.

About fifteen seconds later, I felt a hand on my shoulder. "Nikolas?"

It was one of the Queen's thugs—a man I was actually intimately familiar with, as I'd sucked his cock as part of my 'be a good boy for the Queen and get information' joining pack. He was under six foot, which meant I had a slight height advantage, but he definitely had a width advantage, and a muscle advantage. Considering I'd also got to know him a little less carnally after that particular incident, I was claiming a win on the personality, although I wasn't sure that would be enough of an advantage in a fight.

So far, he was just looking at me, so I went for the standard, "Yep?"

"She'd like to see you."

"She could have just asked normally."

To give him credit, he shrugged. "Orders, Nik."

"You can appreciate that I don't really like this very much. How much shit am I walking into?"

He held up both hands. "No drugs. No torture. On my word, Nik, someone just wants to talk to you."

I heard the car coming down the road towards us, and met my friend's eyes.

And then I nodded.

***

We were driven round the back of an area that I knew, and down an alley behind a strip club—not one that I frequent, I should add—before coming to a stop. I followed the thug, while another got out of the car and brought up the rear. I did seriously debate cutting and running, but well…it was a weigh-up of the two options; shit now, or possible shit later. On balance, I was going for shit now.

We went in through the back door of an anonymous building, down a carpeted corridor, and then the thug opened a door. I was guided in, and there was a woman waiting…a woman with sky-blue hair, bright eyes, and a worried expression.

Sky. My girlfriend.

99

"You fucking idiot," she said to me, standing. "Why the fuck did you think that running away from commitment was going to solve anything?"

I was in a small room, decorated simply—and, if I was any judge, part of the Queen's domain. Sky's fairly relaxed attitude certainly told me that we weren't in enemy territory.

But even if I was on semi-friendly turf, I had to get myself out of this one.

I really wanted to ask what she meant about commitment, but I didn't. There was a puzzle here somewhere, a trap, and I was going to play along until I knew what was happening.

"Was the kidnapping really necessary?" I asked, sitting down meekly on one of the chairs scattered around the room. The thug was still behind me, and I fully expected someone—or several someones—to be listening in.

"Sweetheart," Sky said, and I felt my heart speed up. It was one of our codewords, and it meant everything was about to go south, fast. "You don't walk out on a job with the Queen. You're only alive because I told her everything, and told her it was my fault, ok?" Her bright eyes stared into mine, and she managed to look genuinely contrite. "I'm sorry for pushing you for commitment. It wasn't fair of me. I know you don't want to be tied down with anyone...I just get scared, ok? I need to know that you love me."

I let my breath out. She'd just told me that I was in serious fucking trouble, but she'd bought me some time—and considering that I was alive and intact, it had worked.

I went for contrite too. "I'm sorry, hun." I saw the faint flicker in her eyes. I was playing and we were in this together, on the same page. "You did scare me. I know I should have talked to you, but…I just…"

And I buried my head in my hands.

Sky was kneeling in front of me in an instant. "Nikolas… I'm sorry. It'll be ok. Just keep talking to me, ok?"

Aka. The Queen got the serious heebie-jeebies over my vanishing act, so don't run off again. Don't go silent. You can't afford to.

"I just had a big commitment crisis, you know?" I said to the floor. "I feel like I've got so many other responsibilities, and they're all pulling me, and then you want me to spend so much time with you. I should be spending so much time with everything else. It scared me, hun. I just didn't know how to cope with everything."

Her hands tightened fractionally on mine, and I knew she was getting my message. "You're going to have to pull it together, sweetheart. We've got a job coming up, and it needs both of us. You've gotta get it together."

So there was no way the Queen was letting me out of the Mardos job. Not without broken legs, or a bullet in my back. She wasn't going to let me lighten my workload. So much for that problem crossed off my list.

I raised my head and managed a smile. "I'm sorry, hun. I'm so sorry. I do love you. I just feel split in two, you know?"

She put her hand on my cheek, managing a smile for me. "I know." I kissed her, and then she stood up. "I'll see what's going to happen now."

And she left me alone in that small room, wondering how the hell I was going to talk my way out of trouble from two fronts.

My week was getting better and better.

But Sky returned ten minutes later, and jerked her head from the doorway. I got up and left, following her along the corridors in silence. We knew better than to talk until we were out in the relative anonymity of the streets, where I'd been only a little while previously.

But instead of turning towards my flat, Sky led me the other way and down towards the river. I followed her in silence, and waited as she paid for a cheap room in one of the tiny, tucked-away hotels that littered the city's back alleys.

It was only as we went up the stairs that I asked, "Why here?"

"No one bothers bugging rooms for sex noises."

I knew I wasn't likely to get anything else out of her, so I just followed as we hit the landing and headed up another flight. And, truth be told, I was feeling sorry for myself. I'd been told to get myself into the middle of a major gang without them suspecting me, and get myself out of my current association with the criminal world…and now the Queen wanted me to continue assisting with a major heist against another of my, ahem, employers. And I had to dump the girl whose rather nice ass I was following up a third flight of stairs. Fucking great.

Sky waited until I'd stepped into the room and then shut and locked the door. The bed was clean, at least, even if the room was plain. There was a window that looked out over some dingy rooftops, a vinyl armchair, and a light with a wonky shade. Classy.

"Well?" I asked, turning.

But Sky had taken herself over to the bed, and now sat cross-legged on the end. "Strip," she told me.

"What?"

"Strip."

I rolled my eyes and started pulling my coat off.

"Slowly."

Despite my bad mood, despite my grumps, I felt something stir inside me. I loved it when she ordered me around—I was usually the dominant one, and I fucking loved it when she told me what she wanted. And she was watching with a faint smile, taking me in, enjoying the sight.

I slid my other arm out of my coat and tossed it on the vinyl. My shirt was next, but I took my time with the buttons, teasing her by sliding the fabric down my chest and then back up. I occasionally did strip-teases for my other lovers, but there was something in Sky's expression that made it hot for me as well as her. She always looked as if she was making a list of exactly what she wanted to do with each body part, and my imagination filled in the blanks.

I got my jeans off and then turned my back on her, sliding my boxers down to give her a nice view of my taut ass before turning to display my very obvious erection. She was smiling, and stood up to walk over to me.

But just as I thought I was about to get a kiss she pushed me down onto the chair. I let her, feeling the cheap fabric rub against my naked ass, spreading myself out for her as she looked down at me. And then she knelt between my legs, pushing them apart.

All I got out was "Yes..." as she took my cock in her mouth, and I just let myself go, sprawled on the chair with my head tipped back, everything focused on that shaft of pleasure between my legs. She had her hands on my hips, and her lips and tongue were circling and darting and pulling me in. Even I couldn't get those feelings when I touched myself, and I knew every sensitive spot. She just had a way of hitting everything that just—just—

My hips bucked up against her once, twice, and then she somehow made everything pulse all over again, drawing the orgasm out just when I thought it was over. I realised I was staring at the wall behind me without seeing it, my head tipped back against the chair. She really did make me lose all sense of place.

And then she straddled me, pinning me to the chair, my still-sensitive cock clamped between her thigh and mine. "So?" she asked me, leaning her elbows on my shoulders and looking down into my face.

I was trapped, naked, wrung out. She'd pulled my bad mood out with that orgasm, and I didn't want to fight her. "What was with the kidnapping?"

"The Queen thought that you were trying to up and leave on me." Sky's mouth twisted in bitter amusement. "She's rather fond of me, apparently. She picked you up and told me to sort it out. So I did."

"Seriously? She did that because she thought I was skipping out on my girlfriend?"

"Seriously. She's a bit worried about what you've got yourself into with the Jacks, but that was why she nabbed you." Sky leaned one finger down and poked my nose. "Why were you cutting and running?"

"Can I get somewhere more comfortable?" I asked. "This might take a while."

***

Actually, the move to the bed didn't help. I owed Sky a fuck and I was already naked, so it was only a matter of taking her clothes off…

And then I could plant kisses down her neck with its faint bulge, down her smooth chest, down into the tangle of hair between her legs and up the shaft that reared out of it. Sure, Sky was an unusual girl, but I really liked that. Plus, if I flicked the top of her cock with my tongue just right—

Oh, yes, that groan; the really deep, drawn-out one that told me if I kept doing what I was doing, she was going to make a mess of the bed. It made me hard just hearing it, and it meant I'd definitely keep doing what I was doing.

She came in my mouth, gripping the sheets with one hand and the other tangled into her sky-blue hair. I traced my way back up her stomach and chest, and then planted a kiss on her sweat-salted lips.

"You definitely need more practise at that," she told me, opened her eyes.

"Oh, do I? Would you be volunteering for that?"

"I'd like to see you with someone else," Sky said thoughtfully. She's always refreshingly honest about her desires. "But I'll volunteer for the time being."

"That's very charitable of you."

"I'm a sucker for punishment."

"Oh?" I traced a hand down her shoulder and onto her chest, and circled a nipple. "Are you?"

A pinch brought a gasp, and she ran her tongue over her lips. "Yeah."

"Up for another go?"

"I didn't bring lube."

"Damn. Well, I'll just make you watch."

I pinched her other nipple, making her writhe, and then put myself between her legs. She was watching me with that same appreciative expression, and I made sure I put on a show for her. After all, she liked watching me as much as I liked her watching.

Let's just say we made the most of the room before we got round to talking again.

"So?" she asked me as we lay panting together, a mixture of sweat and semen and lust coating both of us.

"So what?"

"Something happened. Gonna tell me what?"

I stared up at the cracking paint on the ceiling and wondered what on earth it was stained with. Someone had got fluids up there?

"Nikolas…" Her tone should have warned me, but I was tired. Next thing I knew, she was sitting on my chest, her knees pinning my arms and her own arms folded across her chest as she glared down at me. "Talk to me."

I gave up. "They want me to get into the Jacks, soon." Now I was staring at her face instead of the ceiling, with its short nose and faint shadow across one side of the jaw where she hadn't managed to shave close enough. "And they want me to dump you."

She sniffed. "They don't trust me?"

"Not at all." Something occurred to me. "Who told them that I was involved with you?"

"You haven't exactly been subtle," Sky commented, not moving.

"I didn't expect them to be watching that closely."

"Are they?"

"Not that I spotted, but…" I flopped my head back against the pillows and groaned. "I figured that if I was going to get into the Jacks, I needed out of the Queen's stuff. I didn't think she'd take it that badly."

"She can get over-protective."

"She doesn't suspect?"

"I don't think so. You'd be dead if she did." Sky has a suitably blunt way of putting things.

"All right." I sighed. "I've got to dump you. And get into the Jacks while still working for the Queen. I don't need this shit…"

She leaned down and kissed my nose. "If they want you to dump me, does this mean they're cutting me off?"

"I don't know," I admitted. "My boss is the one paying you, and it's her boss that wants me to dump you. I'd have to check with her, but…"

"Bugger." Her shoulders slumped.

"I know." I'd got Sky onto the Angel's books as a way to get her a regular paycheck so she could save towards her dream. If that was gone, then she might go back to her former method of getting money—which had either been stealing or gambling. Neither of which I was entirely happy about.

"Well, you only have to look like you've dumped me," Sky said practically. "We'll just sneak. That's easy enough."

"You live with me."

"I'll move out. That should help to convince them."

I wriggled my shoulders and she let me go, sitting back onto my stomach. "I don't want you to move out."

"It's the most practical option."

I sighed and trailed my fingers up her cock where it rested against my skin. "I need to figure this out."

"One thing at a time."

My fingers stroked down again, and then back up. "Well, I know the first thing I'm going to do."

***

With her usual directness, Sky dumped my problem straight on Benny as soon as we got into his room. We'd had dinner at a nice, private location which doesn't tolerate spies—just to stop any potential problems—and then I said I had business to attend to. She'd tagged along, but if I'd known she had an ulterior motive I'd have left her at mine...

Bah, who was I kidding. Sky always had an ulterior motive. Usually to do with fucking me.

"...move out," I hear Sky finish as I shut Benny's front door and headed into the main room.

"You could live with me," Benny said to his screen, not looking up. He was obviously in a vaguely extrovert mood. Benny in introvert mood kept his door locked and barely talked to me even on text.

I leaned against the doorframe of Benny's bedroom. "You hate people living with you."

"No, I hate you living with me." Benny isn't subtle.

Sky turned to look at me, grinning. "You two lived together?"

"For about two weeks," I said grumpily. "He's a neat freak." I thought my standards of cleanliness were fine. Benny had disagreed. I got my own place shortly after.

"You like clean?" Sky asked Benny, casting a cynical eye around the bedroom with clothes strewn everywhere.

"Clothes are ok. Food isn't."

Sky was looking thoughtful. "A month's trial?"

"You going to bring your system?"

Sky snorted. "Of course I am."

"System for what?" I asked, feeling lost.

"Gaming. We've been playing together for ages."

"Wait, that's what you've been doing?" I said, incredulous. "I thought you—"

"Were doing undercover work?" Sky rolled her eyes. "I gotta chill occasionally. I can't fuck you all of the time."

"Yeah, about that…" I looked at Benny.

"Don't leave mess around," he said, not looking up from the screen. "I don't mind noise."

"Cool."

And that was sorted.

Now I just had the rest of my mess to sort.

Of course, that was the point my phone rang.

Chapter Three

Half an hour later, I was several blocks away and in a lift rising up to Tanya Mardos' penthouse suite. It may have been past midnight, but she was horny and wanted a fuck, and I was the one she called. And let's be honest, being on-call for sex isn't exactly the worst thing in the world.

Tanya's penthouse is, naturally, on the top floor of her favourite tower block; it's actually a relatively short block, which means she's overlooked by an entire square of offices, penthouses and hotel rooms. Not what every mafia don wants, but then Tanya is a little different—and she's got her own vices that entirely suit being overlooked.

I got past security and into her suite, and stepped quietly into her bedroom. As usual, the blinds were open on the large wall of windows, but this time the spotlights were on—shining up from the floor and down from the ceiling, making the darkness outside press in against the sheets of glass. The bed was mostly in shadow, along with the wide desk I knew was there.

Tanya herself was standing in the spotlights, entirely naked, with her hands running down her body. She spotted me in the reflection as I shut the door and smiled.

"I like to think they watch." She lifted one hand and blew a kiss out to the darkness. "They can see me and watch as I finish. You will go behind," she added.

I'd already tugged off my t-shirt and found a condom in her desk drawer. Tanya was running her fingers between her legs, slick with juice, and as I stepped out of my jeans she sucked each finger slowly, drawing them out of her mouth as if every drop needed to be savoured. She'd given me a few blowjobs, and while her posing rather got in the way of the job at hand, as it were, her mouth did feel good.

She turned as I approach; I was already hard and rolling the condom on. While I hate the bitch, she looked good enough to get my libido going.

"You will fuck me," she told me.

"Not yet," I told her from the darkness, waiting to step into the spotlights. "I want to show you off."

She liked it when I took control, as long as it was for her benefit—and this time was no different. As I stepped into the brightness of the spotlights, she turned her back to me, wriggling her ass against my hip. I lifted both of her arms and pinned her wrists against the glass, and then ran one hand slowly down, across her stomach, around the curve of her waist and ass. Then across the front of her thigh as one finger brushed her shaved mound, back up across her stomach, then around the curve of one breast…

"Oh, you torment me so," Tanya moaned theatrically.

I tweaked a nipple. "Your wish is my command." She's got large breasts and I cupped one, catching the nipple between my thumb and finger and gently rolling. It made her weak at the knees, and she was already moving back against my hips and erection.

I moved fully behind her, resting my cock snugly against her ass and bringing my other hand down, cupping both breasts to play with the nipples as my tongue ran down her neck. My hands found her hips, and I slowly pushed my cock into her until I was all the way in, my hips against her rounded ass…then back out, still slow, until the tip was only just in there.

Tanya was moaning at me.

"I want you to scream," I told her. "I'm going to be so slow, and you're going to leave your hands there. I'm going to touch you, but not until you're ready, not until you're so wound up you're begging. Then you're going to come for me."

"Yes, yes," and I slid in again, slowly, gently. And out. She loved this—being exposed under the glare of the spotlights, casting brilliant white light on every part of us, high above the rest of the world in the darkness outside. We didn't know what eyes were out there, watching this show, watching this woman throw her head back and moan as the man fucks her from behind.

In reality, the glass is one-way—security, if nothing else, dictates that she can't put herself on show like that. But illusion is everything, and to us, the darkness was our audience.

I slid a hand around as Tanya's wetness coated my balls and gently touched her clit. The response was immediate—her cunt tightened, and she groaned loudly. Luckily for me her security is used to this, otherwise I'm sure they'd think someone was being murdered.

"Yes, yes! Touch me! Please!"

I did, sliding in and out, teasing and flicking at her clit. She'd still got her hands on the glass but her head was hanging, everything pushed back towards me, begging me to thrust harder and harder as my fingers struggled to hold their position. And then she threw her head back and screamed, and I could feel her clench around me as she shook, her fists hammering on the window.

I withdrew as her spasms tailed off, and waited for her to stand upright again. She's not a cuddly person, and she's also not usually satisfied with one orgasm.

"There's champagne in the fridge," she told me, brushing hair from her forehead with one hand. "I will go and tidy myself. You pour."

I did as she asked, removing the condom and throwing it into the bin first. I hadn't come, but I dislike leaving a condom on when my cock's going down and up. She's rich enough to be able to afford plenty, anyway.

She came back out a few minutes later with brushed hair, but still naked, and flicked one set of the wall lights on to give a gentle glow. I'd poured champagne, and she took the glass casually. I tuned the next few minutes out, nodding and smiling—Tanya likes talking about herself, and it's never interesting.

And then she put her empty glass on the desk, slid a hand down towards her wet pussy, and gave me a smirk. "Now, we go again?"

Chapter Four

I crawled out of bed late the next day with a different set of problems on my list. No coffee was the first, although that was easily solved. The lack of Sky and her ability to deal with my morning erection was another, although a shower and my hand made short work of that.

Next on the list was starting work on my new assignment, which meant I needed more information about the Jacks. I also probably needed to spread around an explanation for my aborted flight, because Jim had been involved in that...

Well, I'd definitely fucked up there. Sky was right, I'd been a prize idiot. For someone that prides themselves on a level head in a crisis, I'd definitely panicked.

Had it been the suggestion that I stop seeing her? Maybe my official boss was right. Sky was obviously affecting me, and she was a liability...

But then how to explain that Sky had been the one who got me in with the Queen? Who had taken the risks to get me into the world I was in? Who'd been called a freak for me?

I sighed. It was something to think about, but right now, I had to work. I needed information.

I arrived at Benny's apartment after stuffing a pile of grease between doorsteps of bread down my throat—otherwise known as a fried egg sandwich—to find Benny and Sky in his room, one in his chair and the other on Benny's bed, playing Halo.

"Jeez, you two. Work to do?" I grumbled.

"We did it," Benny said without taking his eyes off the screen.

"Already?"

"You wanted a plan," Sky said, also watching the screen. "We have one. You've already kicked me out, so that'll convince the angels that you've broken up with me. Next, you need to get more information on the Jacks. Benny and I are going to help you, and then when you have a huge success with them, you'll credit us. That will convince the police that I need to be paid again."

"Is it all about the money?" I grumbled, trying not to be irritated.

"Yes."

I sighed and sat down on the end of Benny's bed, next to my girlfriend the devoted player. "It's not that simple. Taking down the Jacks isn't going to be easy."

"Get me in there," Benny said. "Same as before."

"I don't have anyone in there."

"Jim," Sky said, looking away from the screen for a brief

moment. By the time she looked back, it was too late. "Bugger, I'm dead."

I borrowed her before she could restart, pinning her arms in a hug and covering her cheek in kisses. She laughed and surrendered, and as she kissed me deeply, I felt my cock stirring in my jeans. It had only been a day since she'd moved out, but I'd missed her.

As her hands started down my chest, I managed to regain some awareness. "Uh."

"He doesn't want to do it," Sky said, her hands still going downwards. "He doesn't mind watching."

"How the fuck do you know that?" I managed to get out, between concern for my partner and the rather overwhelming desire she was causing with her fingers on my crotch.

"I asked."

"It's fine," Benny said from the chair. "Just don't get sweat on me."

Sky obviously had no intention of doing that. She pushed me down on the bed and knelt between my legs, undoing my jeans as she did so.

Benny was happily playing Halo, and I had to admit I was hard. Sky's lips encircled the tip of my cock and began to slowly push down—

"Oh, fuck, I can't..." I pushed her off. "Sorry, but this is just way too weird."

"Somewhere else?" Sky raised an eyebrow at me, but did sit back on her heels.

"Uh. Look, I'm...I could use a coffee," I said in defeat, and pushed my cock back into my jeans as I stood up.

Sky stood up as well, and smiled at me. "All right. Let's go and get a coffee, and I'll tell you about our plan."

***

As it turned out, their plan was simple. I say that, but...

I just had to worm some information—and invitations—out of Jim. Great.

I let my hands absorb the faint residual warmth of the coffee mug, and blew out a sigh. We were on Benny's ragged sofa but I didn't dare risk getting fluids on it, so sex here was out too. "I need to know more about them, really."

"Well, you've got a contact," Sky suggested from the other end of the sofa, her foot stroking up and down my leg.

"True." I considered it. "I just don't know if he's going to actually talk to me about them."

Sky fixed me with a long stare and got up. "Even you think it's suspicious that he's been hanging around you for six months and hasn't probed. Maybe you need to take things to the next level?"

"Doesn't that usually apply to relationships?"

"Well, it is. You're not talking about the big stuff, so start talking."

"Except in this case, it's his job..."

"Just text him." My girlfriend had obviously given up on me as a source of sex, and was heading back towards the game. I made a mental note to make it up to her. She'd have to sneak into my apartment...I couldn't really spend too much time at Benny's, otherwise it would be obvious I hadn't broken up with her. This might take some thought.

***

"She told me that she loves me!" I groaned to Jim later that evening. We were sitting, not unsurprisingly, in a pub. I'd shifted our fortnightly drinking session with the excuse of wanting to vent about my girl troubles, and I was doing some damage limitation by spilling out my 'worries'. "She wants to move in with me! I just…freaked, you know?"

Jim was quiet as always, listening. He got a bit more vocal when he'd had a few drinks, but considering he was pretty quiet anyway, that only brought him up to normal levels. "What's the problem with living with her?"

I groaned again. "It just…it just scares me, you know? I'd have no problem with a housemate, but…she's gonna fill my sofa with fluffy cushions, or something."

"She's not an ordinary girl," Jim pointed out, slightly uncomfortably. We'd had several discussions about Sky; Jim was not happy about trans people, but was happy that I was happy. He seemed to cope with the fact that I was semi-serious with Sky, at any rate.

"To make it worse," I said, ignoring his comment, "I could really use a housemate. The apartment's awesome but the rent's gone up again. I don't want to move, and if I do move, Sky'd want to live with me. I'm screwed whatever I do!"

Jim coughed. "I guess it's an appropriate time to bring it up…"

"You've got a girlfriend?" I suggested with only moderate sarcasm.

"No. I'm being evicted from my place. The landlord's moving his girlfriend in."

"Oh." Then my brain made the connections. "You wanna live with me?"

"It crossed my mind." Jim can be blunt when he needs to be. "I promise not to fill your sofa with fluffy cushions."

It was possibly the stupidest thing I'd ever done on a whim, but it solved a lot of my problems. "I'll get you a lease."

We may have spent some of the rest of the evening eating bowls of noodles and drinking. The noodles soaked up the alcohol, but that doesn't mean I remember much of what we talked about. Jim had relaxed enough that he talked shit with me too, although I do remember that he told me he was gay. That stuck even through the mild alcoholic glow.

I left at close to midnight, and let the walk home sober me up. When I got into my house I found Sky sitting in the middle of my bedroom floor trying to work out which clothes were hers.

"Jim's moving in," I told her, plonking down on the bed.

"What?" I hadn't seen Sky look so horrified. I did wonder if she'd throw the shirt she was holding at me, but she settled for dropping it into the suitcase. "Nikolas, he's a Jack! I know I said to get close to them, but are you insane?"

"You work for the Queen," I pointed out, and leaned back on my elbows to watch her continue packing.

She rolled her eyes and picked up another shirt. "You invited him to *live* with you…you've got no idea what he's going to find out."

"Pot, kettle."

She glared.

"I got Benny to look into him when I first took up with him," I said. "Ex military. No convictions. Works for them because he's happy shooting people, but he doesn't have a record on their systems either. Does his job, goes home." I hesitated, and then said, "And I *like* the guy, Sky. We've spent six months drinking together. He's a good man, even if I am trying to get into his…"

"Secrets." She sighed. "Ok. I've gotta trust your judgment, baby, but sometimes I seriously wonder if you got dropped on your head as a child."

She only called me 'baby' when she meant 'idiot'. My glare deepened.

"We're not going to be able to do as much," Sky said mournfully after a moment, and I relaxed. She'd accepted it.

"We'll make time," I promised, and walked over to pull her into a hug.

There's something wonderful about sex with someone you've been with for a while. You know how they tick, what works, what will make them smile or groan or writhe.

For Sky, it was when I pushed her fingers around the bedframe, and told her to keep her hands there. She didn't like the restraints of bondage, but to have to obey, when it was only her self-control keeping her there? I loved driving her to the edge of distraction, kissing and licking up her body and back down again, teasing the head of her cock and then swallowing it into my mouth, pinching her nipples and then oh-so-gently tormenting them…

And then I could use her, smear lube across her ass and cock, slide my own hardness up against hers and then press against her tight ass, pushing my way in, spreading her legs and watching as she opened herself to me, wanting to be used and fucked and brought to the edge of orgasm again and again…

I came inside her, her legs wrapped around me. As I relaxed, I smiled up at her, her hands still clenched firmly around the bedframe. "So, you want to come?"

"Yes."

She was so hard, her cock dripped onto her stomach. I ran one finger up the shaft and made her groan. "I want you to beg."

"Nikolas, you bastard, make me come. Please."

"That's not begging."

"You know I want to. You can make me come, I love finishing in your mouth. Let me come. Please. Please."

I pulled my cock out of her and shifted myself down the bed so that my head was level with her cock. "You want my mouth on you?"

"Yes. Yes!"

Her cock was twitching, and I touched the swollen tip with my tongue just to see it move.

"Please! Nikolas. Please. Let me come. You felt so good and I just want—"

Her words dissolved into a moan of pure pleasure as I slid my mouth onto the salt and sweat, down to the curls of hair at the base and back up. It only took a few strokes before she was begging again, thrusting up against my lips and tongue, desperate for release.

I kept her there at the edge for as long as I could, but I could feel her orgasm building. And then a few quick flicks of my tongue on the tip and my mouth was filled with salt as she spasmed against me.

I swallowed, licked the last of her cum off the tip of her cock, and walked around to sit by her head. "You can let go now."

She opened tired eyes to me, smiling faintly, blissful and exhausted. I unpeeled her fingers from the frame, kissed her nose, and went to clean up. By the time I got back, she was asleep.

I watched her for a minute, trying to appreciate how she'd made such an impression in my life. Sky-blue hair and a wicked grin. Who would have suspected that she'd steal my heart?

And then I shoved her over, made sure she was wrapped in half the blankets, and drifted off with one hand on her warm shoulder.

I'd known she was a thief, but I guess I didn't mind too much what she stole.

Chapter Five

As it turned out, Jim moved in the next morning. At 9am. When you've been up until 2am fucking your girlfriend, you tell me that's a decent hour. Luckily, Sky had left about half an hour before he rang the doorbell, so I didn't have to worry about my ostensibly-ex-girlfriend appearing. However, I'd gone back to bed after she left, determined to make up on my sleeping time, and hadn't anticipated my new room-mate interrupting it.

I managed to open the door without yawning and found the small, shaven-headed man waiting with his usual bland expression. He had two suitcases and a duffle bag, which looked fairly incongruous in my nice hallway. I helped him haul everything in and then waved a hand. "Coffee?"

He came through, eyes darting. He'd taken the lease on trust, having never been to my place, and walked around it with wide eyes. "This is nice," he murmured as he returned to where I was waiting impatiently for the machine to brew my lifeblood.

"Enjoy it," I told him. "It's partly your money that means I stay here."

That made him smile.

"Half the fridge is yours. Coffee's there. If you drink all my nice stuff, buy more. Beyond that, I don't give a fuck what you do."

He gave the polite cough that meant he was going to bring up something difficult. "How often is Sky over? Do you, uh, get noisy?"

"We'll tone it down," I promised. "We're not noisy, honestly. If it gets too bad, say. I'll find the gag."

I saw him swallow and look faintly disturbed. In some ways, I was flattered. His default expression when he was working was a polite, blank mask. To get any reaction out of him meant that he trusted me.

"Joking," I told him, and got the flash of a smile that meant he was relieved.

I guess that was something I wasn't going to admit to Sky. I trusted Jim, for all that he worked for the Jacks. I liked him, too. We might still end up on opposite sides of the game and potentially even trying to kill each other, but for what it was worth, he was my friend.

I got him sorted in a room, gave him the spare key and went to get dressed, wondering if I really had let a snake into my life.

Well, he wouldn't be the first.

***

125

I got back from my errands as it got dark to find Jim sitting at the small table, eating something out of a packet. I dug food out of the fridge and we had a pleasant conversation about nothing while I cooked, and then another pleasant conversation while I ate. It was just…nice, you know? The sort of thing that doesn't need any thought or stress. It was like the relationship I had with Sky, except without the sexual tension. Or work stress.

But hey, I'd take any amount of problems for the chance with a girl like her, especially when the sex was that good.

I suggested that we move into the lounge and watch some crap TV, and went to get changed out of my work gear into a scrappy pair of tracksuit bottoms and a t-shirt. Jim agreed, and reappeared a short time later in a surprisingly smart pair of pyjamas. He also had four bottles of beer, and we got on with the pleasure of being able to drink without having to leave the house.

"So," I said after a while, knowing that I'd have to start somewhere. "How d'you end up working for your bunch of bastards?"

"They aren't bastards," Jim objected, strongly for him.

"Could have fooled me. Isn't that why you're keeping the gay thing a secret?"

I might have been imagining the flash of panic, but I'm used to Jim's deadpan expression. There was definitely something there.

And then the deadpan returned, and he shrugged. "The Jacks don't care who you fuck."

"You don't fuck anyone, though." I was happy to divert the topic off to something else, and if it meant I could capitalise on Jim's unease to put a few more cracks in his veneer, great. "You've never even mentioned a partner."

"I don't like being close to people." That had to be the beer talking.

"What, physically?"

He shrugged.

I eyed him for a moment. He was cute, sure, but not really my type…although considering Sky is my type, she's definitely spoiled me for everyone else. But Jim's reluctance said something else to me: not that he didn't want to be around people, simply that he hadn't really had the experience.

I felt like I was stepping off a cliff, but that's when I live. I said, "Come and cuddle."

"What?" It was definitely the beer's fault that he didn't walk out, which is what I was counting on.

"I've got a girlfriend," I told him deliberately. "I'm not romantically interested. You're fucking lonely, you're too deep in your own shell to break out, and you need some human contact. I'm going to put some bad TV on, and we're going to watch it. That's it. Come here."

I saw the hesitation, and deliberately turned to find the remote. When I'd found it, Jim was sitting next to me, beer clutched in one hand and the deadpan expression definitely underlaid by nerves.

I settled myself back against the squashy cushions and tugged a stiff and reluctant Jim onto me. He's smaller than me, so he fitted quite well with his back against my chest and his shoulder tucked under my arm. He didn't have to look at me.

It took about half an hour for him to relax a little, but I

could feel him slowly easing down from the nerves. This was ok. This was good. Human contact didn't mean some half-dressed prostitute in a dirty room, or whatever shitty situation he'd had previously. I wasn't going to ask and he wasn't likely to tell me, but the least I could do was make him a bit more comfortable with actually fucking touching other people.

And getting a hug from a friend. That's just human comfort.

***

It was three evenings later when he mentioned a word that made everything click. Asexual.

That was also the evening he told me about one of his previous encounters. I admit I winced quite a lot. Fucking a prostitute can be fun, sure, if that's what you want. But when your so-called friends buy it for you and then try to pressure you into it…urgh.

I'm all for sex, but it's gotta be on your terms.

"It often isn't," Jim commented when I tried to express that.

"Well, no." I tried to consider a world with no sex. Or, no, wait, no sexual attraction. "So other people can have sex, right? You're not, like, anti-sex?"

Jim shrugged, his shoulder moving against my chest. "It's just another form of exercise. I don't find it arousing."

"And you've never had…feelings?" I squinted at the TV. "Do you even masturbate?"

"I think that's a bit too personal, Nikolas."

I squeezed his shoulder as an apology. "Just trying to understand. It's a bit of an odd concept for me, you know?"

"Considering the amount you fuck," Jim said dryly, "I can

entirely see. I just don't get the urge."

"Maybe you just haven't met—" I started.

"Nikolas," Jim broke in crisply, despite the two beers he'd had, "it has nothing to do with attraction. I like me. I like people." I noted the correction. "I'd be entirely open to a relationship. I just do not get excited about the idea of smushing my genitals against someone else's."

I had to laugh. "Ok, you win. Asexual, no interest in hanky-panky, but into mushy romance with the right person."

"Exactly." He relaxed a little.

"So I can still set you up on dates?"

"I can assure you," the gun-toting, lock-picking, tiny badass of a motherfucker that I was currently cuddling said, "that I am not any kind of potential dating material."

I grinned down at his shaved head. "Hey, there's someone out there for everyone."

***

Which is possibly why I blew up quite so badly a week later, when Sky and Benny told me what they needed. Well, it was what Benny needed—apart from being told when he's a pissing ball of shite. He needed the same sort of access into the Jack's network as we'd previously got for the Queen and Tanya. There, it had been a case of Sky spending fifteen minutes with a server, and my sticking a USB into Tanya's laptop to give her a helpful little virus in between sexual sessions. But this...

"I can't get in!" Benny snapped at me. Benny doesn't ever snap, even when I left food dishes all over his ultra-tidy kitchen. He was looking pretty upset—but then, I was pretty upset too.

"He's my friend!" I could hear that I was close to yelling, and tried to bring my voice down. "I won't hack his laptop! That's not fucking fair!"

"They don't have any other points," Benny said, his tone coming closer and closer to a whine.

Sky stepped in at that point. "Nik, let's go talk about this in the other room."

I knew she was diverting me, and I let her—Benny's a pain in the butt but he's also my friend, and I was very, very close to ruining that.

"It's not fair to him," I said to Sky as we got into her room. She had a nice big double bed, and not much else in there—not that I was particularly interested in anything other than the argument at hand.

"No, it's not. Neither's life." Sky's got a way with words when she wants. "Benny keeps getting blocked. He needs physical access, and we don't know any other locations. They're hackers, Nikolas. They're not stupid."

"Then how do you know putting something on Jim's laptop is going to work? Isn't he going to have protections?"

"Yes, but it's a physical point. Benny can try to get through them then."

I glared at her.

"Take it or leave it," Sky said unsympathetically.

"What if I left it?"

"Then find us another way in."

"Look, that was why I wanted the guy to live with me—so I didn't have to break in to anything!" I snapped. "I'm working on this, Sky. He's just starting to trust me, and if hacking his laptop goes wrong, I throw all of that away!"

"You've got to get in somehow! This is the only thing we can come up with." She was frowning at me.

"I need some more time, and—"

"We don't have time, Nikolas. Either think of something else or just do it."

I turned and walked out.

Chapter Six

It was cold, raining and dark by the time I got back to Benny's place, and Sky met me at the door. "Hey."

"Hey yourself," I said, stepping in. "I'm sorry I was grumpy."

"You're allowed to be. Benny did some thinking and—"

"I've already done it," I interrupted. "Went home, used the one from Tanya's hack. It installed. See if Benny's got access."

Sky vanished, and I took off my coat and shoes. I'd been walking around long enough, trying to get rid of my grumps, that I was cold and wet. I wasn't happy about the decision I'd made, but it was the best one I could think of under the circumstances.

"It went on," Sky said, appearing from the hallway.

"Cool. Shower?"

She took my hand and we headed for the bathroom.

There is nothing quite as blissful as a really hot shower when you've had a few hours out in the cold being a philosophical grumpy bugger. The heat of the water on my skin was painful for a few moments, and I groaned.

"Hey, wait for me," Sky said, and her naked form slid in beside me. I was hard by the time her arms wrapped around my waist and I pushed her against the tiles, water cascading over our heads and shoulders, soaking us in steam and spray. We kissed, tongues pushing against each other, fighting for control as our hands tugged at hair and nipples. It wasn't gentle, but I didn't want to be. I wanted her teeth against my shoulder, biting hard, the sharp contrast of blossoming pain with the heat of the water, the pinch of her fingers on my balls followed by the stroke of pleasure up my shaft. I wanted to fuck her mouth, tangle my fingers in her hair and feel her lips and tongue and throat around my cock, push her against the tiles with my fingers curled against her neck, her hands digging into my ass and groans muffled against my cock—

I came into the heat of her mouth, overwhelmed by the torrent above me and drowned by the pleasure below, resting my head against the tiles as the rush subsided and everything began to ache.

A hand reached up and flicked the shower off, and Sky said, "Are you ok?"

"That…was…"

She slid herself up my body and got my arm around her shoulders, manoeuvring me out of the shower and into the steamed-up chill of the bathroom.

"Wow." I met her eyes and reached up to touch her cheek.

"I didn't hurt you?"

"No." She smiled.

"You'd tell me, right?"

"I always tell you. You know that." She grabbed a towel from the rail and wrapped it around my waist. "I like you using me. I trust you."

"I trust you." I don't know how the words escaped from my heart but they were somehow on my lips and out, into her mouth, into her eyes and ears and sky-blue hair. "I love you."

She met my eyes and smiled the most perfect smile, through heat-flushed cheeks and messy blue hair. "Nikolas."

"I do." I tangled my hand in her hair again, pulling her head forward to kiss her forehead. "Sky. I love—"

It did choke me the second time, and Sky stopped me talking with a kiss.

She didn't say it back, but that was ok. I knew she needed to take her time.

***

The next week went past pretty quickly, between my errands for the Queen, fuck-dates with Tanya, evenings with Jim and snatched meetings with Sky. Occasionally I had a meet with a contact in the Angels, but mostly it was just encrypted shit. Whatever Benny was doing, it wasn't anything useful to me— and so I just got to carry on with my life.

And another week trundled past, until:

"We're in."

Sky's sometimes got a warped concept of timing. I paused, my cock just pushing at her asshole, the clenched muscles slowly opening for me. "I'm not yet."

"No, the computer access." She was on her hands and

knees, and turned her head to look at me over her shoulder. "To the Jacks. Benny got into their mainframe."

"And you're telling me this now, why?" I started sliding again, my lubed cock pushing slowly into her ass.

"Because...I forgot...when you arrived." She let out that wonderful, deep groan that told me I was doing this right, and I dug my fingers into her hips as I began to slide out again. "I got distracted."

We'd left a trail of clothing through the apartment, I realised with a guilty wince. Benny would probably be grumpy. "So, you want me to stop?"

"No!" That was a groan of almost agony, and I couldn't stop my own twin groan of pleasure as her muscles contracted around my cock, pulling me in. "Hell no. You're going to finish this."

"Finish me, finish you, or both?"

"I want you to fuck me so you come," Sky said, flopping down onto her elbows and burying her face in the cushions as her ass pushed against me. "And then I finish."

"Of course." I let my fingers trail up her smooth back, along the ridge of her spine, tickling at the crease of her ass where it curved into the base of my cock. I loved fucking her ass—either slow, steady, gentle, or hard and fast and panting. Which option?

I went for option three, which was a steady pace and a handful of lube down under Sky's hips to slide onto her cock. Sure, she'd told me to come first, but I like to make her happy.

I matched the pace of my thrusts to my hand, slowly speeding up, watching the body in front of me tense and move, thrusting backwards to meet my hardness. I liked being behind as it let my balls swing, adding extra sensation—and because it meant I got to watch her grip the pillow and gasp into it, muffling her groans as she re-lubed my hand.

"You haven't come yet," she managed to pant, turning her head in the pillow.

"Are you sore?"

"Not yet."

"You want to be the other way up?" I pulled out, moaning as I did so—I was painfully hard—and Sky flipped herself onto her back, wrinkling her nose as the puddle of cum on the bed smeared her skin.

"You'll need to change the sheets anyway," I told her, pushing her legs apart, and slid into her ass again. "Oh, you're good."

"Come kiss me." She tugged my head down, and played her tongue across my lips as I picked up my stride again. Sky always knows exactly how to turn me on, and her hand in my hair, the other running down to my ass, her body moving against mine—

She bit my lip as I came, panting into her mouth, pushing into her body as everything overwhelmed me.

"Fuck, I needed that," I said, and pushed myself up onto suddenly wobbly legs. "Shower?"

"Yeah, then talk to Benny?"

"Oh, the hack!" I winced.

"See, you forgot too!"

"Yeah, ok. You're distracting." I slapped her bare ass as she rolled off the bed.

"Says you!"

A quick shower, and I went to see Benny.

"Yeah, I got in," he told me.

And this is why Benny earns enough to sit and play computer games most days. He can't cope with an office, won't ever work in a team, and doesn't like people—but if you want sneaky code that snoops around, he's your man.

I don't really get it apart from that, but it's not my field. I talk to people. And…well, fuck people.

I left my spot by the door and sat on his bed, watching the lines scroll down the screen.

"They're fighting me," the hacker said briefly.

To me, it didn't look like anything—just moving colours. He had one of his screens covered in the scrolling lines, and a second one covered with open windows, all either displaying webpages or odd snippets of text. The middle one was black, with coloured writing, and he was hastily tapping away.

"I got some moles in," Benny said. "They've found a few of them. I think they've got a team. Their code's patchy."

"Any locations?" I asked hopefully.

"No, it's all being redirected."

"Damn." There went my chances of taking anyone out manually. "Do you—"

I was interrupted by a sudden flurry in the scrolling lines, and Benny snorted. "You're trying that? Really? Amateurs."

His fingers were already flying again, and I leaned my head back against the wall to watch. It was a battle that I couldn't understand, even if I could see the fighting: the defences, the sallies, the blows and the misses. Benny hit a key and paused for a second, watching a box.

"Gotcha," he muttered. Then his fingers were off again and a second box filled up with text, was sent and begun again.

"They've missed two," he said to his screen, and with a start I realised he was talking to me. "I gave them a decoy and they've gone for it. I'll let them think they've won and—hah, there." The text was suddenly rolling up the box again. "They've nuked that one. Good. Let me just shore up some defences and I'll start getting you the information you want."

"How do you learn all this stuff?" I asked, bewildered.

"Practise. Same as you talk to people. Now shut up or go away, Nik. I'm busy."

I grinned at my friend's back, and went to do what I do best—talk to people.

***

Two days later I was out, at a bar—a local, where the barman knows me. He's one of those grumpy gits who apparently hates everyone, so I have no idea why he became a bartender. That said, he's good at his job—which isn't really bartending.

As I took my drink—which had spilled down the sides— he stayed opposite me for a moment. "Bearded, grey shirt."

That meant someone wanted to meet me, and he'd just told me who it was. I knew he wasn't going to tell me anything else, but I tried anyway. "Why?"

The grumpy git just shrugged and moved on to the next customer.

I took my drink back to my friend, who had somehow gained a young woman to drape around her. How she does it, I don't know. But it did give me the chance to take a sip of my pint and look around the pub. I couldn't see anyone matching that description, so I just sat and drank.

About ten minutes later, in walks a man: broad-shouldered

with a grey shirt and a suit jacket over the top, jeans under, boots beneath that. A curious mix of casual and smart that he somehow pulled off. I realised I had let my gaze linger for a little too long, and picked up my half-full pint as cover. His beard was a full-face reddish one, but neatly enough trimmed that I could see his lips underneath. Full eyebrows that probably did a good glower, and a head of red-brown hair. The sort of man who just quietly walks through life, getting what he wants by sheer force of presence.

And he wanted to talk to me? I frowned internally. He'd be affiliated with someone.

Well, hopefully for my continuing paycheck, it would be the Jacks.

The man got his drink, and then headed straight over to my table—and I realised he was carrying two pints. He nodded to my friend—still mostly engrossed in her girl—and then to me. "Care to join me, Nikolas? I got you a bribe."

I had the dizzying sensation of my heart leaping at the same time that my stomach plummeted. He knew who I was —somehow—and the way he talked to me was so absolutely familiar that I wondered if I'd met him before. Had I? I was almost questioning my own sanity as I absently checked on my —oh yeah, she was set. There was kissing. I followed the man to a table the other side of the room, and took the pint as he slid it across. "Thanks."

"I'm Bear." He had an engaging smile, a smooth and low voice, and very dark brown eyes. I wasn't sure if I liked him: there'd be a razor blade in there somewhere, I was sure. He was just too damn nice. Too friendly. "Thanks for this. I've been wanting to have a chat to you."

"What about?" I asked, not caring too much if I sounded blunt.

"Your work."

I took a sip of the pint, wondering if it was spiked. Well, it wouldn't be the first time I'd been drugged, and I knew Sky was meeting me here later. I just had to stay in the pub and not say anything stupid. "You want extra help?"

"In a way." He took a sip of his own pint and wiped the foam off his moustache. "We're interested in some of your…" He made a face as he thought, and I tried not to smile. If nothing else, Bear was personable. "Friendly skills."

"You want me to chat someone up?"

"In a way."

I get sick of conversations where people dance around the details, and this was no exception. "Lay it out."

"I work for the Jacks."

And there was the razor blade. Well, at least my guess had been right.

And then my stomach dropped again. Benny had got access to their files yesterday, and started to pull out a whole wealth of information—did they know? Were they laying a trap for me?

Well, only one way to find out.

"Ok?" I said.

"Your work with Tanya Mardos hasn't gone unnoticed," Bear said.

"You want me to seduce someone."

"A trial run, if you will."

"Who? And what's the actual assignment?" I asked, and then added, "And what's the pay?"

"We give you more assignments—"

I held up a hand. "Nuh-uh. Actual pay. I don't need this." I felt like a git, but sometimes you gotta be. It's like that artists and exposure thing. It doesn't pay the bills. "And I don't really like doing trials. I know you have to check I'm ok, but you wouldn't be talking to me if you thought I was shit. Either I do decent work, or I don't take the assignment."

Bear was silent for a moment, and I wondered if I'd pushed it too far. And then he burst out into laughter. "You make a good point."

"So who's the target?"

"Hi Nik," a voice interrupted from behind me, and Sky kissed my cheek. "Hi, Bear. Haven't seen you for a while. How's cat?"

"She's just fine," Bear said, a smile lighting his face, and went off on some story about what I eventually decided had to be an actual animal. Chasing string and getting stuck behind the sofa didn't sound like something a human would manage. Sky had taken a chair and was listening with an adoring expression on her face, and I wondered if I should get her a kitten.

Bear finished his story, drained his pint and turned to me. "So, tomorrow night for dinner?"

"What?" I spluttered.

"The Blue River, 8pm." Bear winked at Sky and stood.

"When did I agree to have dinner with you?" I demanded as he walked past my chair.

"See you there," was the only response I got, and then he left the pub.

"What the..." I turned back to find Sky grinning. "What?"

"He likes you."

"He works for the Jacks," I muttered.

The smile slid off her face. "Bear?"

"Yeah. Asked me to take on an assignment."

The shock was wearing off, and she made a face. "Damn. I didn't guess that one."

"Makes you wonder what skills he's got for them."

"So what did he want you to do?"

"He didn't get round to saying. You interrupted."

Sky made an apologetic face. "Well, apparently you're going to dinner with him…"

"Yeah," I said, draining the rest of my pint. "Yeah."

***

"Off out?" Jim asked the next evening, looking up from the table as I strolled past the kitchen door.

"I've got a date," I told him. "Do I look ok?"

"Smart." Jim came over and undid my bow tie. "You don't do this often, do you?"

"No," I admitted, breathing in his scent.

"There," he said, and stepped back. "You're good."

"Thanks." I gave him a wink and sauntered out.

Now, I'm not usually a patron of the Blue River's type of place, but I know how to behave. Stroll in, don't act nervous, pretend you could buy everything in sight, and everything will just fall into place.

As it was, I was escorted across the half-full restaurant—with its white-clothed tables and chattering diners, each with their own multiple wine glasses—and handed over to my bear.

He stood as I approached, and held out a hand. He was in a full suit, a dark grey with a waistcoat and a dark shirt that

142

somehow worked despite the muted colour. "Mr Jinsen, you are looking very stylish."

Ah, so it was going to be that sort of evening. I shook the hand, liking the cool of his palm, and said, "Thank you. I don't often scrub up but I hope it works well."

"Indeed it does." He gave me a smile that twitched the beard, and we sat down.

I knew what he wanted, but I have to admit he was good. The questions were woven into the conversation, subtle and charming, but all the while trying to tally my cover story with whatever they'd found out. What was my past? Who did I work for? When had I arrived in the city? And the razor blade lurking amongst the sweetness: did I work for the Angels?

I diverted most of it by being honest—in a way. I had grown up in a shitty area. I used to work for the gangs. I had slid myself up to the grey areas, but I didn't mention that it included an agreement to work for the Angels. And I diverted the rest by using the tactic that had worked so well last time: I talked about Sky.

Well, and cats.

We spent all of the main course on cats. Apparently I shouldn't get Sky a kitten, they cause havoc with electronics: a house-trained adult is the way to go. We discussed breeds, adoption, toys and food, intermingled with stories about Bear's cat.

I'm not usually one to go gooey-eyed over pets, but seeing Bear's face light up as he talked about his cat was just adorable. And I'm saying that about an almost-six-foot bearded man.

It was cute.

We'd had desserts before I got round to asking about what

he'd actually invited me here for: a job for the Jacks.

Well, a test assignment. Bah. But as long as they paid me, I didn't care.

"The assignment..." Bear said thoughtfully. "You'll need to go and see Fan. She'll give you a target, and a challenge."

I got her number, and—with a smirk that I knew would make him smile—Bear's number. He tucked his own phone back in his pocket, pushed his empty chocolate-smeared plate away, and looked me in the eye. "I don't suppose you'd be interested in a nightcap?"

I was, I admit, surprised—and flattered. But then when a blonde woman hadn't been able to seduce me while drugged, and I had a known fondness for cock, it was an obvious morsel to dangle. "I'm flattered, but I don't do one-offs."

"Ah." He smiled, not at all bothered. "Well, thank you for meeting me. It's been an interesting evening."

I shook his hand, left him at the table, and took myself back out to find a taxi. The cold air sobered me, and I found myself drawing in deep breaths as I tried to make sense of it all.

I'd just been wined, dined and romanced. Wow.

Chapter Seven

Sky howled with laughter when I told her about the evening, and didn't stop giggling even when I told her about the assignment. "I didn't think they'd have a sense of humour! That's great!"

"You're not bothered about me having assignments to... to...be a sex toy?" I asked, not sure why I was irritated.

She took a breath and sat up, wiping her eyes. "Nikolas, you know it doesn't bother me. As long as you're safe, and you're not in love with them, I don't care. It's what you chose to do."

I couldn't pinpoint why I was annoyed, but I was.

"Would it help to make a scene?" Sky jabbed me in the chest with a finger. "If you don't want to take the assignment, then don't. If you're worried then don't go. But I'm not going to be jealous and stop you."

"Why aren't you jealous?" I asked, aware that I sounded almost plaintive.

"Because I get what I want," my beautiful girlfriend told me, winding her arms around my neck and snuggling into my lap. I shifted her ass against my hips and hugged her. "I get priority. If I want you, I tell you, and you fuck me."

"What about Tanya?"

Sky nuzzled into my neck, and my cock—already stirring from her proximity—began to push against my trousers. "She's a bitch and you hate her. That's fine. I can cope with you fucking her as long as you call her a bitch when you get back."

I had to laugh at that. "All right."

***

And so the next afternoon, I went to see Fan.

"I want you to seduce someone," she said to me. We were sitting in the front lounge of a snazzy hotel; I wondered if the Jacks deliberately picked locations to try to disconcert their marks, or if it was just the obvious place for a meeting to her. The waiter brought cups of tea: not my standard drink, and certainly not when it's in a delicate china cup, but I wasn't going to get myself off onto a bad footing. And so I was sitting in a comfy chair opposite a middle-aged, dark-haired woman dressed in a slightly unflattering blouse and definitely impractical shoes. I did a mental contrast to the Queen, and decided that I liked my pseudo-royal boss better—if only for her sensible attitude to everything...except Sky. Those protective instincts could get annoying.

I focused back on Fan, and tried not to sound impatient. "Yes. Bear said. Who do you want me to seduce?"

"Bear."

I thought I'd misheard. "What?"

"Seduce Bear."

"Did he put you up to this?" I very nearly growled.

She fixed me with a stare. "No. He wanted me to give you a challenge, and knowing your history with Tanya, I want to see how you'll approach it."

"And that's the assignment? Make him orgasm?" I might have been a little snarky.

"Are you going to take it or not?" She proved she could snark right back.

"No." I matched her, stare for stare. "As I said to Bear, I don't need these jobs. You're fucking me around if you think I haven't spotted what you're on to, because he's obviously put you up to this—or it's some kind of practical joke. I'm not playing. Either make me a serious offer, or I'll go away and pretend I don't know you."

Her mouth was pursed, and I wondered if she'd take me up on it. And then she let out a breath, and in the tone of a peace offering, said, "Would you like another cup of tea, Mister Jinsen?"

I nodded, and let her beckon the waiter over. We sat in silence while the teapot was taken away and brought back, along with some more cakes—which I admit I was eating most of. Fan poured more tea, and then I waited in silence for her to restart.

"He's lonely," Fan said to me as we sat with our fresh cups of tea. "And when we learned about you, he was interested. He's the one who's been following what you've been up to."

I took a sip and let her talk.

"You're a good operator, I'll give you that. Getting into Tanya's cunt isn't hard, but staying there is something no one else has managed."

Interesting. Tanya hadn't let that particular nugget slip.

"You've made friends with Jim, who isn't very sociable. Apparently the Queen likes you, although I take that with a pinch of salt." Ah, there was history there! "In short, your skillset is one we'd be interested in for our operations."

I decided that silence and an interested expression was the best option.

"Bear proposed the test; you'd have to seduce someone, and do something while you were there. Plant something. Steal something. Just a trinket, but something that's obviously a little more difficult to do than if you just break in."

"Wouldn't it be easier to just break in?" I asked.

"We already have that skillset. I want proof that yours can be turned to what we need."

I sighed. "And Tanya isn't proof?"

"Like I said, getting into her cunt isn't difficult."

Well, at least they didn't know about Benny's little hack and my fun with the USB. "So, why Bear?"

She took another sip of her own tea and put the cup back down before speaking. "He's lonely, and he's interested in you. He won't be expecting it from me: there are other targets I should send you after. Other challenges. But I want his dry streak ended."

"What's the assignment, then? And the pay?"

She named a figure, which I considered and then nodded. "And the challenge…a cork. A wine cork."

"Does he drink wine?"

She shrugged. "I have no idea." And then she smiled at me —a slightly smug smile, tinged with satisfaction. "Is that enough of a challenge for you, Mr Jinsen?"

"Does he know?" I asked. "How do I know this isn't some elaborate set-up?"

"You don't." It was flat and chilling. "But if I wanted to blackmail you or him, I have plenty of other material. Take it or leave it, Mr Jinsen. That's your ticket to working with us."

I pushed my teacup towards her and stood. "I'll let you know."

***

"Only if you tell me all about it afterwards," was Sky's only proviso as we sat together that evening. "And I don't think it's a set-up. I mean, it could be, but…he hasn't been with anyone for a while. She's telling the truth there. And he did like you."

"You're such a romantic," I grumbled. "I'm still worried it's a set-up. I'm going to be butt-naked and they're going to jump out at me, or…"

"They haven't done anything since," Sky said quietly. She knew I hadn't forgotten being kidnapped and drugged when the Jacks first wanted information out of me. I wondered who had come up with that plan.

And who had come up with this one.

Well, either I won or I lost, and this was my chance to get in. I pulled out my phone.

Bear answered within two rings. "*Nikolas! This is a pleasant surprise.*"

"I changed my mind about that nightcap, if the offer's still open," I told him.

"*Why the change of heart?*" He sounded a bit surprised.

"I can't stop thinking about you." And actually, it was true. I wanted to know what he was like in bed. How far down that beard went. What was under that suit. What he looked like when he came.

"I thought you didn't do one-offs?"

"Sky wants to hear all about it afterwards."

I heard the bellow of laughter down the phone, and then he came back on the line, still chuckling. *"Well, I can't disappoint her, can I. When?"*

"What's wrong with now?"

Forty-five minutes later, I was getting out of a taxi at the foot of a tower block. Ten minutes had been picking up a bottle of wine that I liked, wondering if he'd like it, checking with Sky—who told me she didn't have a fucking clue and I'd just got her killed, which meant she was playing something with Benny—and going back to my original choice. And now I was here, looking up at the lit windows above me and thinking about Tanya's exhibitionism.

I'd wondered about getting a hotel room, but Bear had invited me over and I'd accepted. It meant if there was a trap I was walking into it, but then a hotel room had a veneer of anonymity that I didn't necessarily like. Sky knew where I was going, and had offered to come and rescue me if needed—and that meant she could potentially bring both the Queen and Tanya's resources down on someone's head. Tanya Mardos didn't care about much in the world, but I figured she'd probably have something to say if her current sex toy wasn't available on demand.

And so I headed for the main door and pushed the button for the flat intercom.

"*Yes?*" Bear's voice said almost immediately.

"Nikolas."

"*Come on up.*"

He was waiting with the door open when I came up the fourth flight. I'm always grateful to my exercise routine that keeps me in shape—and lets me perform as expected. Sky is always helpful with it, too. It's astonishing how many positions I need to fuck in to keep my muscles in check.

But I pushed her out of my mind and smiled at the man in the doorway. "I brought a present."

"Oh, nice." He was definitely more interested in me. "Come on in."

I followed him into an open-plan kitchen and living space, with two huge squashy sofas and a relatively tidy work-surface. "I'd guess you don't want food?" Bear asked.

"Nah, I ate. How about a corkscrew, though?" I asked, pushing my advantage.

"Sure." He pulled one out of a drawer and then spent a moment staring into a cupboard. "Uh. Wine's not usually my thing, so I don't have any glasses…"

"Whatever's good," I told him, unscrewing the cork from the bottle and taking it over to the bin. A clang, and I'd 'thrown it away'. There, job done.

Far too easy.

Bear turned back with two pint glasses. "Ya think these might be too big?"

"You don't need to get me drunk, you know," I told him, smirking.

I got that roar of laughter again, and it made me smile. He let go when he laughed in a way that made me wonder again what he'd be like when he orgasmed. "Well, here's to you, then."

"Are you sure you wouldn't rather a different drink?" I said ruefully. "I'm guessing you don't like wine if you don't drink it?"

"I'm always open to new stuff."

I couldn't resist. "Oh, really?"

He blushed. He actually blushed. "So. Uh, you want a tour?"

I got a showing of the apartment—which actually helped quiet my fears of an ambush, as there wasn't anyone hiding. The cat was asleep on his bed, and merely opened one disinterested eye at me when I stroked her head. Bear apologised to her, and suggested we sit on the sofas for a bit, which I happily agreed to. I took my half-pint as far as the coffee table, and put it down. As I stood up again, he was just putting his glass down at the other end, and—

Well, it was too good an opportunity to miss.

Half a step and I was almost up against him. He was only a little shorter than me, so a head-tilt was all it took to bring my lips into contact with his. He was uncertain, hesitant—and then just as I was worried that I'd overstepped, his hand moved around my waist, his mouth opened, and his tongue slid out against my lips.

I ran one thumb over his beard, loving the unusual sensation. It was soft; he obviously took care of it. I wondered what his bush was like. Just as soft? Hopefully I'd get a chance to find out.

I had no idea how long we spent kissing—long enough that my lips were getting sore from the unexpected friction of the beard. Bear pulled back and gave me a smile. "So, uh…"

"I want to make you finish," I told him, "and then we can fuck. Deal?"

"Yeah." He relaxed against the sofa cushions. "Deal."

He watched me as I undid his jeans and slid his cock out of his boxers. He wasn't as big as I was expecting—thankfully—but he was thick, and dark, and circumcised. The head was swollen already and leaking, and I wanted to lick it off.

"Condom?" I asked him.

"Oh, yeah. Wait a sec."

He stood up, not bothering to tuck his cock away, and headed off into the bedroom. He was out again a second later, holding the box.

"Saves time later," he joked.

There was a bottle of lube in the box too. "Sensible," I remarked, tearing a condom packet open. Bear just grinned, and then the expression dissolved into something closer to wonder as I deftly rolled the condom onto his cock.

"Oh," he said. "Yes."

"Watch me." Maybe some of Tanya rubbed off on me, but I know when someone likes to see what I'm doing.

Bear's eyes fixed on my face, and I kept his gaze as I lowered my mouth to the tip of his cock. It almost leapt between my lips, but I made sure I took it slow, just to keep that desperate, yearning expression on his face for a little longer.

And then I took as much of him into my mouth as I could, sucking down and back up. There was no way I'd get anywhere near the base, not with him being as thick as he was—my mouth already hurt.

Hand job it was, then.

"I'm sorry, I'm kinda big…" Bear said, almost apologetic as I gave the tip of his cock a flick with my tongue.

"Means I get to watch you while I jerk you off," I told him, and picked up the lube. A handful of that and his eyes almost rolled back in his head as I slid it up his cock.

"Oh, god…" he groaned.

"Watch me," I told him, and he refocused his eyes on my hands. "You like?"

"Yes." He was already panting, his cock twitching in my hands. "The tip—yes, there. Yeah. Just…just—yeah."

I slid a thumb around the base of the head, teasing the ridge, loving the way my fingers could get right under it. I haven't really encountered many circumcised lovers, but it's always fun to try new things. Running back and forth seemed to really get to Bear, and he uttered another panting torrent of moans. "Yeah, yeah, that, just…oh god, yes…"

I didn't bother encouraging him; I just watched his face as it went from helpless desire to desperation, needing the release that I was pulling him towards. And when he finally came, it was with a panting cry and a jerk that violently filled the condom with white.

"Oh, god…" Bear groaned as I took my hands away. "Fuck."

"I'm just gonna wash," I said, and headed for the kitchen. It took Bear a moment, but he pushed himself up and got the condom off, and then came over to throw it in the bin and wash his own hands. He was sweating and red-faced, but gave me a smile, and took the remainder of the wine back over to the coffee table to top up our glasses.

We sat on the sofa for a bit, drinking wine and chatting about TV, games, bars—usual, normal stuff. He didn't bring up work, and so neither did I. It didn't seem like the right place.

He hadn't put his cock away, and after about half an hour of wine and chat, I could see it stiffening again.

I finished the last of my half-pint, and gestured at his crotch. "So what's next?"

He put his own glass down. "I want to see you." He sounded almost shy, nervous. "I want to fuck you."

"Here?"

"The sofa's had worse."

I don't usually bottom, but that's because Sky loves it—and I like making her happy. But I'm definitely not averse to it. I pulled my t-shirt over my head while Bear undid my jeans, and then we squirmed and wriggled and I was naked on his sofa, the leather cushions under me and Bear's weight on top, horny as hell. All he had to do was lower his head and I was kissing him, our legs tangled together and his beard rubbing against my face, his tongue pushing between my lips in a way that was making my hips thrust. I pulled away, panting, and found him almost as breathless as I was.

"You," I told him and began to undo the rest of his shirt buttons. He helped, revealing a chest covered in the same reddish-brown hair as his face, and then pulled his still-undone trousers down. I just watched, leaning up on my elbows, my body bare and smooth in the golden lighting and my cock showing just how badly I wanted the man now naked in front of me.

He caught me watching, and smiled. "So?"

His chest-hair continued down across his stomach and joined with the mass of curls around his cock. I looked him down, and then back up, and caught his eye.

"I want you to fuck me," I told him. "I want you to come inside me."

His cock jerked, and I could see the desire overtaking his nerves. He pulled a condom out of the box and rolled it on, his fingers shaking slightly, and then grabbed the lube and knelt down between my legs.

"I don't want to hurt you…"

"Then go slow." I turned myself over, pushing my ass up towards him, and felt the cool drizzle of lube go down my crack. After the warmth of the sofa it was a shock, but a good one; and my cock was now against the warm material, smooth and silky.

Bear's finger slid in, and I gasped.

"I'll go slow," the man murmured, and I spread my legs as he pulled me further onto his lap, lifting my hips and gently pushing his finger back in, opening me. I buried my face in the oiled pillows and let him tease me, pushing in and out, filling me and then withdrawing, pushing in again with another finger, spreading me wider and wider as he pushed in another and another—

And then I heard him groan by my shoulder, and his body was against mine, warm and rough, and his hips met my ass. "There…Nikolas. There."

"Fuck me," I told him.

"You…I don't…I'm not hurting you?"

"No." He filled me tighter than anyone ever had, but the slow build-up meant I didn't hurt. I felt pinned, held in place by the tightness and pleasure mixing. "Just go slow."

He was gentle, and he was slow—painfully, agonisingly slow, a tease and a torment that had me moaning into the cushions. And then he was tugging my elbow, and pushing my hand down to my own cock. "Finish yourself. I want you to come."

"Your sofa…" I managed.

"It'll clean." He sounded hoarser, and I wondered how much self-control it was taking for him to go slowly. Had he ever been able to fuck any of his lovers without hurting them?

I began to stroke, and heard a deep groan from behind me. My ass had tightened around his cock and I was holding him, feeling every thrust and twitch of him inside me. He began to fuck me again, unable to hold back the lust. His hips slammed into mine again and again, pinning me against the leather, my cock clenched in my fist and my ass filled with him, pushing me so close with every stroke—

I came, gasping into the cushions, my whole body jerking. He was still thrusting into me and I could feel him getting closer, tense and urgent.

His fingers dug into my hips and he gave a queer little moan, almost hurt—and then pulsed once, twice, a long third stroke that started his legs shaking. And then he subsided against me, his head on my shoulder, pressing me down into the leather with a long, panting sigh.

We lay there for a long minute, me just cataloguing the aches and the pleasure, feeling his cock still twitching in my ass and his beard smooth against my shoulder. Then Bear stirred, and said, "Sorry, Nikolas, I'm squashing you."

"Not to worry." We got ourselves disentangled with a few

smiles, and then Bear directed me to the bathroom to clean up. When I came out, the cat had woken up and come to investigate—and when Bear came out in turn, he found me butt-naked on the second sofa with a cat sitting on my clothes, purring madly.

"She obviously doesn't want you to get dressed," Bear joked, looking entirely at ease in a pair of boxers and nothing else.

"Obviously," I said, and picked her up. "C'mon, sweetheart, I have to go and tell Sky what I've been up to."

Bear laughed and took the cat from me. "So, um. Thanks."

I did up my jeans and smiled. My ass was starting to get sore, and I knew I'd ache in the morning, but it had been worth it. "Where's your cleaning stuff?"

"Nah, I'll do it. Seriously."

I shrugged. "Ok." I pulled my t-shirt on, smoothed down my hair, and gave him a raised eyebrow. "So, you've got my number if you need it."

He nodded, and I could see a blush start again under the beard. "I…I might well do that. If you'd like."

I stepped closer to him, giving the purring cat a scratch with one hand, and kissed him deeply. "Yeah."

He escorted me to the door and gave me another of those bashful smiles as I left. I was still smiling as I headed down and out.

I made sure I got round the corner before I pulled the cork out of my pocket, clicked a photo and sent it to Fan.

Round One to me, bitch. Bring on the next one.

***

I had a couple of days of silence from the Jacks—and from Bear—after that, but I didn't let that worry me. I had errands for the Queen, an assignment with Tanya, and I managed to sneak a meeting with Sky...

Well, I turned up at Benny's to check on progress, and she was there. That counts, right?

"I've got a meeting..." I told her as she wound her hands round my neck and began to kiss up from my shoulder.

"Just a quickie?" She took my hand and dragged me towards her bedroom.

"You know I love quickies." I let myself be dragged, grinning. As we got into the room I glanced at the clock. An hour to go, that'd be fine, it would only take me ten minutes to walk.

She tugged me onto the bed after her, and we spent a few minutes just cuddling, heads together and bodies touching. It was one of the things I missed about not living with her, and while I loved the sex, the closeness was nice too.

And then she said, "Will you watch me?"

I turned onto my side and kissed her cheek, her lips, her hair. "Do it."

She's so fucking sexy when she touches herself—I loved watching the way her fingers move, the fact she touches herself so differently to the way I finish her. I like long strokes, and so does she—but when she gets herself to come, she rubs the head of her cock, teases it, strokes it. It's fascinating, and having her panting and moving next to me, biting her lip, makes it even hotter.

I had my lips on hers as she came, moaning, and I stroked down her smooth stomach, patterned in wet salt.

"You haven't come yet," she said as I handed her some tissues.

I glanced at the clock. It seemed like longer, but I was still good. "Where do you want me?"

"Next to me."

I turned onto my back and Sky's hands pulled my shirt up, exposing my stomach. I liked her jerking me off, but there's something simple about doing it yourself. I do it differently, too: Sky knows I like long strokes, but she does it slowly, teasing. I race myself to the finish, desperate to just tumble over into that—

It was almost painful, a jerking pleasure that left me gasping.

"Hot," was Sky's only comment, and I kissed her nose. She dumped a tissue on my stomach and I got as much of it as I could. Damp stuff, sticky and escaping.

When I flopped back, Sky wound herself around me. I glanced at the clock again. Half an hour...I could stay here for a minute, sure.

Sky wound her legs around mine and rested her head on my shoulder. I ran a finger down her face, and then started playing with her hair. "I'm glad you're growing it out. I like it longer."

"Something to hang on to?"

"You got it." I reached down and squeezed her ass. "And that."

"I like it when you do."

My phone buzzed, and I disentangled myself enough from Sky to reach it. A message from the Queen about a job—

Wait, what time?

"Your clock's wrong!" I pushed myself up, dislodging Sky. "Seriously? I told you I had a meeting!"

"You didn't tell me when!" she protested.

"I'm already in enough trouble by screwing you!" I was frantically pulling on my boxers and got one leg into my jeans before I realised they were the wrong way around. "Now you're screwing up my job too?"

"I didn't mean to!"

"For fuck's sake!" I pulled my t-shirt on, grabbed my coat, and ran.

***

I headed for the meeting point feeling out of breath and extremely grumpy. I was late, but considering I'd left the house fifteen minutes after the actual meeting time, of course I was late! My contact only ever waited ten minutes. I was screwed.

I slowed as I approached the junction, though; it wouldn't do to arrive flustered, and I needed my wits about me, even if I was meeting someone I knew in a usual place. The Angels might not be that imaginative, but when something works, they stick to it.

I took a breath, let it out, and started to stroll up towards the main street. And stopped.

Someone had just walked past the end of the street: someone I knew.

A Jack contact.

Coincidence?

I pulled my phone out as if I'd just got a message and leaned against the wall. I could look like I was texting, and keep an eye out from under my hair…

And I felt that odd little shiver go down my spine again as the same person walked back the other way, heading down the street.

If I'd been here on time, I would have been sitting in a cafe, catching up with my Angel contact.

Was someone on to her? And had wanted to check me out, too?

Things were clicking into place.

I didn't think I'd been seen, but I headed back the way I'd come anyway. I didn't want to risk getting any closer to the meeting point.

So, now what?

I turned towards home, and when I got in, left my coat and shoes on. I knocked on Jim's door, and when he answered, I said, "I want to meet your bosses."

Chapter Eight

We were in a bar: no customers, chairs on the tables and pint glasses neatly arranged in clean rows. It was mid-afternoon, and I'd been the last to arrive. Bear and Fan were waiting for me, with Jim and another woman I didn't recognise. Bear stayed sitting at one end of a long table, and gestured me to sit to one side, with Jim opposite and the woman at the other end. Not quite us against them, but close.

I don't know what exactly Jim had said to them, but Bear opened the conversation. "Nikolas, I know you're interested in what we think of you." His voice was smooth and low, all honest concern. "We have doubts about where your loyalties lie."

It was all razor blades with this lot, wasn't it? I raised an eyebrow. "You know I deal with a lot of dodgy folk. Which particular connection had you worried?"

"The police," Fan said flatly.

I got the impression from the Bear that he wished she hadn't been that blunt, but his eyes were still on me. I just gave her a long stare.

There was a moment of silence.

"So?" I said. "Are you going to back that up? Give me any more information? Tell me who's been suggesting it so I can punch their lights out?"

"You're not denying it," the woman snapped.

"I've sold them information before, when the price has been right," I snapped back. "I give them the bastards that fuck children, because that's easier than murder. What about that bothers you?"

"You could sell anyone out."

"So could anyone." I gave them my sardonic smile. "That's the point, isn't it? Pay me enough and give me enough incentive, and I won't sell anyone out to anyone else. At this rate, the Angels aren't interested enough in you. The Queen, however, is."

"We're interested in her," the Bear murmured.

I shook my head. "I don't sell information between the people I work for. I'm in too many pies for that. I only sell to the Angels because they're not fucking anyone else."

I saw the Bear nod, understanding, but the woman's face was still pinched. "You admit that you work with the Angels."

"And someone's hinted to you that I'm a double agent," I filled in. "Can I make an educated guess for you at this point, and suggest that they have an ulterior motive?"

I was right: Fan's eyes flicked across the table.

"I might have found out something about that person

which you don't know, and they don't want you to know?" I ploughed on relentlessly. It was starting to look like my guess was right. "That means they don't want me here, working for you?"

More eyes were turning to Jim.

"So?" Bear asked me.

I looked over at Jim.

I was right. He'd been after me as much as I'd been after him, and now he knew that I was possibly a threat…he was trying to push me out.

Well, at least he wasn't trying to kill me.

But it didn't mean I could be nice.

"He's gay," I said flatly.

"Nikolas," Jim said, and I'd got through the mask. His voice was shaking.

I stared him down across the table. "You've been so fucking scared of it the whole time. Bear's fucking gay! He doesn't hide it! They—don't—care!"

"However, we do," Fan said bitingly, "care about secrets. Jim. You have opened yourself to blackmail. You're on probation until we get this mess sorted out." Then she turned to me. "You're on probation as well, Mr Jinsen. We'll be in touch with you."

Jim was just sitting there, the mask back on, but I could see his nostrils flaring. I wasn't sure what to say.

But Bear nodded, and I took the cue to leave.

***

"Did you know the Jacks were trying to ambush me?" I asked Sky an hour later. I'd gone for a run to work off some stress, and then gone back via Benny's. Benny himself was out on one of his infrequent errands, but Sky was on the patched sofa, reading a magazine with words like "hardware" and "gigabyte" on the cover.

"I suspected."

"Why didn't you just tell me?" I asked, exasperated.

She opened her mouth, and then realised that she'd fucked up.

"What."

"Benny got in to the police files," she confessed.

"He fucking…" I sat down on the sofa. Well, it was obvious that he would have, but… "So you knew who I'd be meeting, and where?"

She nodded.

"Why didn't you just say the Jacks were suspicious?"

"Because Jim was the one who clued them in."

And she thought I'd automatically doubt her if she told me? That brought back all the frustrations of the meeting, and I leaned back with a huff of breath. "Well, that's a fun one too. So, I had a meeting…"

Sky's face got tighter and tighter as I told the story. When I'd finished, her fists were clenched, and she was staring at me with a look that I could only describe as horror.

"You outed him?"

"Well, yeah. It was the only way I could prove he was the one—"

"You…" I'd never seen her so angry. "You utter fucking bastard."

"What?" I was completely confused.

"I don't like the guy, but that's just…" She was shaking her head. "You don't do that to someone, Nikolas. You don't

166

out them. Even if you think it's in their best interest or you've got an ulterior motive or…or…whatever stupid fucking justification you've come up with. That was his choice to make. His choice! And you took it away from him."

"He was trying to get me kicked out, and quite probably killed!" I protested.

"You could have done something else," my girlfriend snarled at me. "You've always got some fucking clever plan. You could have dealt with it without bringing Jim into it at all, and definitely without telling his fucking bosses."

I was shaking my head, but a slow trickle of guilt was worming into my stomach. "I couldn't think of anything else."

Sky shook her head, stood up and headed out of the room. "I'm going for a walk."

"You want company?"

She stuck her head back around the door. "Just leave me alone for a bit, Nikolas. I love you, but I'm too fucking pissed off with you right now."

I heard the door bang a moment later, and slumped back against the sofa with a sigh.

Well. Fuck.

***

I headed back to my own flat, knowing that I'd have to face the situation there at some point. It may as well be while I was already grumpy from Sky, and in the mood for a fight.

Jim was there, and came out of his room as I walked down the hall. He was still in his suit and coat, but I couldn't see the faint bulge that meant he was carrying a gun. One plus for me, I guess.

I faced down my former friend. "Why?"

167

He had his deadpan look on again, the trademark blank face. "They asked me to. They wanted to know more about you since you started working for the Queen." He raised an eyebrow at me, then. "You did the same."

I couldn't disagree. I had manipulated him and abused his trust—although it didn't sound like the Jacks knew I'd got into their files. I'd leave that a secret. But I had been happy for him to move in because it got me one step closer to their organisation.

This was one of the points I hated about being a double-crossing spy. I was supposed to be on the good side. And I felt like an absolute shit.

I didn't ask Jim my next question, though: why not Sky? I knew the answer. Jim didn't think Sky was worth anything: she was a freak, a weirdo, someone too unimportant to even bother with. And that had protected her.

"Why the police?" I asked instead.

"You do work for them."

He had a point. They just hadn't known how deeply. Hopefully, that was another secret I'd managed to keep.

"So what now?" I said.

He shrugged, and started to turn back into his room. "I'll pack up my stuff and move out."

I held up one hand, and he stopped.

"I don't necessarily have an issue with the betrayal," I told him. "I did the same. I outed you without permission." Sky's lecture was still worming into my gut, and I hated the feeling of guilt. "That's just business. If you want to keep living here, you've got to accept Sky."

I had cracked the mask, just a little. He was surprised.

"You don't like her, I get it. But I think most of that's prejudice. Sure, you don't have to be best friends. But she's gonna be around more often, so if you could at least tolerate her getting coffee in the mornings…"

Jim was silent for a long moment, and then gave a short nod. "I will…need time to think."

"You can leave your stuff in the room. I'm not going to rent it out from under you."

He nodded again, walked back into his room, and shut the door.

I looked at it for a long moment, and then turned. I had more bridges to fix.

***

I went to see my boss. The official—and secret—one.

"It's good information," she told me. This time, I'd been invited to sit across the desk: obviously I was more in favour than last time. "Benny's given us the feeds and we're working through it. But we need…"

I waited patiently as she listed details, and then shut the file. "I'll make sure all of that gets over to you in the next few days—"

"Hang on," I interrupted, knowing this was a prelude to You Can Fuck Off Now. "I've got a few things to raise."

She gave me a rather suspicious look.

"My usual agent has been compromised. It's fine," I added pointedly before she could say anything, "just don't use her for anything undercover."

The file was open again and my boss was scribbling. "Compromised? You're sure?"

I sighed. "The Jacks know about her. I don't know who

else does. Just don't assume she's anonymous." I knew they liked having some known police agents floating around—it made it easier for snitches to snitch. "And second, it was Sky who was responsible for finding that out. If she hadn't, I'd be dead."

Another, firmer, scribble. "You want that noted on her file?"

"I want her paid again. And I'm dating her." Deceiving them had been fun, sure, but I wanted a warm body in my bed and peaceful time with the girl I liked. My boss narrowed her lips, and I produced a glare. "It's not negotiable. I've had several other job offers, so you should be grateful I'm still here. I don't think it's exactly unreasonable that you put her back on your books and start fucking trusting her, considering she just saved my life."

A smile, and another scribble. "I'll mention it. Anything else?"

"A pay rise, but I know that ain't going to happen." I pushed myself up out of my chair. "Now, if you'll excuse me, I've got errands to run."

***

I texted Sky with the good news as I left, and by the time I got home, her coat was on the chair by the door. Jim's shoes were there too, and I heard voices as I headed down towards the kitchen.

Jim was sitting at the table with Sky, and they were talking —it sounded like a cat conversation. I made a mental note to get that cat for Sky, especially if she was living here again.

Sky smiled at me as I came through the door. "Coffee's on."

"Nice." I bent over to give her a kiss, and looked at Jim. "So?"

He gave me a small smile, and gestured at the half-empty mugs and definitely empty plate between them. "A short-haired cat, definitely. Long-hairs shed a lot."

"Are you being a bad influence?" I asked my girlfriend.

She grinned up at me. "Bear's got a friend who's got two adults, and they don't get on…"

I rolled my eyes. "For fuck's sake, you won't even let me surprise you with a present? When have you booked to see it?"

"This evening."

I glanced at the clock—one with the right time. "Excellent. 'scuse me," I said to my housemate, hugging Sky to me. "I need to borrow my girlfriend for a bit. We might get noisy."

To give him credit, Jim didn't flinch, and just took a calm sip of his coffee. "I'll buy some earplugs."

BOOK THREE

FOR QUEEN AND COUNTRY

Chapter One

There's something about fucking people I hate that I absolutely love.

It's partly the pleasure. I can make them writhe, moan, plead for me to just keep doing what I'm doing. I can stop, teasing and taunting, sliding in and out slowly, flicking a clit or a nipple with my fingers or tongue. I can reduce them to a begging, panting mess just by using my body and my cock.

And it's partly the sense of power. It's being able to bend them naked over whatever I want, grip their hips, thrust in again and again. I love the way my hips slam into their skin, the way my fingers pinch and tug flesh, eliciting moans of pleasure even when I'm hurting them.

And it's definitely the ability to make them orgasm. I can make them scream and groan, squirt over my fingers or pulse cum over their skin. I can draw it out, getting that build-up oh oh oh! until it snaps and they shake, jerking under me, held by my hands and cock and mouth as they can't control their pleasure.

To see someone I hate at my command, helpless under my tongue, is really satisfying.

Case in point: Tanya Mardos. Blonde, large-breasted, round-assed, and quite frankly one of the biggest bitches I've ever met. She was a bitch to my girlfriend, and she's a bitch to most of the people around her. She's also a grade-A bitch when it comes to business, mostly because she doesn't shy away from the illegal side of things.

She's usually quite nice to me, but that's because I have a cock and I know how to make her come—multiple times, if necessary. I'm a tool that she likes, especially right now, because I've just given her a screaming orgasm in her favourite position: up against the floor-to-ceiling windows of her penthouse, with everyone outside able to see her hot, naked body.

Not that they can, incidentally, because security dictates the glass is one-way. But it's a fantastic illusion, and considering Tanya is an exhibitionist, she makes the most of it.

She'd just finished making the most of it, and headed back into the room to pick up a drink from the desk as I wiped my face and remembered how to breathe. I had my back to the glass, which thankfully meant I couldn't see the height, but having my nose pressed into someone else's crotch wasn't exactly a good alternative. Although her orgasm had been pretty satisfying, even if it had left me with juice all over my face.

I gave my face a quick wash in her bathroom, and came

back out into the opulent room to find Tanya leaning across the desk, still entirely naked, her ass on display.

She looked back over her shoulder at me, and said, "Now you fuck me."

Two orgasms was normal for Tanya so I was quite happy to oblige her, and rolled on the condom she'd left on the edge of the desk. But as I gripped her ass, she opened a drawer and pulled out a vibrator.

Now, I don't come for Tanya Mardos if I can help it. I hate the woman. I enjoy every single furious thrust I can place into her cunt—and, luckily for my job and my standing with her, so does she. But I don't finish for her. There's reasons behind it, but the primary one was that she'd hurt my girlfriend. I didn't forgive that, and that meant I wouldn't give Tanya a single shred of my pleasure.

But I had the large-breasted, blonde crime queen bent over the desk, her gloriously rounded ass pushed out for me, wet cunt just there for me to fuck, the vibrator buzzing against her clit. And as I thrust in, the vibrations were running through my cock, making the head tingle, rushing to my balls. I had to keep going. My orgasm was building, even though I was fighting the feeling, even as I thrusted harder and harder into her.

I hated her so much, but I couldn't fight it. I couldn't stop. I didn't want to stop.

And as she screamed and writhed in front of me I dug my hands into her thighs and pulsed out the bursts of furious pleasure mixed with vitriol and rage, biting down the moan that shook my body.

I withdrew before she noticed, escaping back to the

bathroom as she relaxed back in the chair to recover. I shut the door on her sweaty, naked body and almost ripped the condom from my cock, staring at it in defeated disgust.

It had felt so good. And I hated that she'd done that to me.

I flushed the damn condom down the toilet—I know it blocks the pipes, but there was no way I was giving her any shred of a hold over me. It was a sign of my weakness, and I just wanted it gone.

I had to force myself to go back out, but Tanya was sitting at the desk, still naked, tapping at her laptop with a refilled glass of champagne next to her. She waved a hand as I came out. "That is all."

I made myself nod, collected my clothes and escaped to the other room. As usual, Tanya's servant was there to watch —I think he enjoyed being a voyeur, and I didn't doubt that he masturbated over the videos of me fucking Tanya. But at that point, I didn't care. I just wanted to leave.

I got a taxi back to my flat, trying not to think as I watched the city go by. I felt dirty. Used. Weak.

My housemates were both away for the night, and the house was dark. I managed to shed my clothes and get myself into the shower, trying to scrub away the memory, trying to scrub away the feeling of being abandoned, of having betrayed everyone.

But it had felt so good.

I found myself on my knees, water pouring around me, my cock in my fist and my body shaking from the mix of pleasure and guilt as I came all over again at the memory. It had felt so good, and I wanted it again.

And I hated myself for that.

I crawled into bed, naked and wet, and tried to reassure myself that I'd feel better in the morning.

***

The morning brought Sky, along with a large mug of coffee. I rubbed some of the sleep out of my eyes and accepted the beautiful brew, along with a kiss from my girlfriend.

"So, how was it?" she asked.

I felt like someone had hit me in the gut with memories. I took a swig of the coffee, but Sky had already seen my face.

"What happened?" she asked.

"She used a vibrator. I came."

My girlfriend sighed. "I don't get why you do that."

"She hit you," I growled.

Another blink. I hadn't ever seen Sky lost for words, but I think she genuinely was. "Nikolas…"

"She called you a freak!"

Sky swallowed, and I wondered if I saw tears hovering in her eyes. "I'd forgotten."

"How could you forget?"

And the look that crossed her face broke my heart.

"It's not the first time, Nikolas," said the woman who had been born into a man's body. "And it won't be the last. People think like that. I'd rather ignore it than remember it."

I stuck my chin out. "Well, I've remembered."

"You know the Queen's still after her," Sky said. "But you don't have to do it for me."

"I know. I hate the bitch. Anyway," I added, "I don't like being ordered around."

My slim, beautiful lover climbed onto my lap, pushing me

down onto the bed. "You don't?"

"Not by her. By you…"

"Since when have I been able to order you around?" She was teasing me, a smile crossing her face to replace the too-calm mask. "You usually ignore me."

"You give me unpractical orders," I pointed out.

"Like 'fuck me'?"

"Oh, that one I can do. Is that an official order?"

She gave me a mischievous smile. "Absolutely."

"I hear and obey, oh mistress."

***

I got the lust out of my system—and Sky's—and got a shower, thinking. My original brief from my law-and-order employers had been against the woman who was now my unofficial boss, the Queen. She'd been the one to request that I turn my talents onto Tanya Mardos' organisation, and I'd helpfully fed that information back to the Angels as well. They'd been more than happy to have more juicy stuff on the organisations that formed the underworld of the city, and they'd opened a formal investigation based on what I'd fed back. So…I could see what they were up to, as well as checking up with the Queen. Beyond that, I wasn't sure what I could do. I definitely couldn't go after Tanya myself; she was just too powerful, and I had nothing to go on. But if I could get someone with a bigger clout to move against her…

But sitting across from my boss in the police station, things didn't go as well.

"What do you mean, the investigation's on hold?" I asked. "I specifically got you the second hack because you wanted evidence against her! A month ago it was all going well, and now it's been cancelled?"

"It's just on hold, Jinsen," my boss said repressively. "Not cancelled. Operational reasons."

Which meant that someone up above her had handed the order down and hadn't told her why. Call me cynical, but I found that suspicious. "You don't know anything?"

"No. You're off that side of the investigation anyway, Jinsen. You're meant to be investigating the Jacks, remember?"

"I'm working on it." And I was, sort of, in between everything else. As long as I still got information to my bosses from one of the several areas I was working on, they were usually happy. "Well, I guess you won't need the information on the Queen either, or..."

"The others are going ahead," my boss snapped. "Are you still sexually involved with Mardos?"

"Occasionally."

"You will no longer need that contact."

I stared. "It's a good in, and you want me to burn it?"

She just gave me a glare.

"All right, all right." I didn't have much intention of doing it on the Angel's say-so, but I was starting to wonder what was going on. This was stinking rather more than I liked.

As I stepped out of the station, I began to wonder if I really was too suspicious. Operations got cancelled for lots of reasons, and it didn't always mean something fishy. Could have been money, or manpower...

But then why spend so much time and money to have me —and others like Benny—investigate, and then suddenly shut it down? Why not shut down the Queen and the Jacks too?

Why just Tanya?

To me, that stunk.

I decided to go and see someone who might be able to do something: my current boss—or one of them. If you want something done then go and see the people who'll actually pull a finger out and do it, not just have a meeting about it—or in the Angel's case, blow me off with bollocks about operational reasons. So, I was ambling along, heading for the Queen's pub headquarters, when I had a shiver down my spine.

Someone was following me.

She was obvious enough that I clocked her, and that immediately put her into one of two categories. I was either meant to catch her, or she was a rookie.

She wasn't particularly attractive, which is exactly what you want in a tail. Dark curly hair scraped back, trouser suit, practical shoes. Jacket loose enough to conceal whatever she was carrying, which I doubted was a gun. Handcuffs, more like, which put her more firmly into the police category—and police tails do tend to be pretty blatant. It's something in the way they get trained, I think, plus she was in a suit and it was mid-morning. No office worker would be lingering quite that obviously on the street as I stopped to check my phone and sent a text. Oh dear, what do they teach the kids these days…

For a moment, I was amused. They'd sent their rookie to tail me?

And then I felt the panic set in.

Why the fuck were they watching me, now?

Well, two things to do. One, get rid of my tail. Two, work out why I was suddenly under suspicion.

First things first.

Chapter Two

F ancy a drink?"

I'd continued my amble along to my local establishment...and, incidentally, the Queen's headquarters. It's a nice bar if you like the standard alcohol, although they do have a few unusual ales sneaked in amongst the cans. Everyone's pretty friendly in there, because it's the gateway to a lot of jobs. I liked it.

So I'd wandered there, keeping slow and simple so my tail could follow. I went in the door...and then went back out the back door. At that point, I could have made good my dodge and gone on my way. But my tail wasn't just for today, and I wanted to have some fun.

The way she jumped was pretty satisfying, and I allowed myself the luxury of a smirk as she spun around to face me. "What?"

"A drink," I repeated, still leaning against the wall where I'd put myself, nice and non-threatening. "With me. In a pub. This pub."

She briefly followed my jerked thumb to the sign over the door, and then her eyes flicked back to me. Dark eyes, too, to go with dark brows. She had too much foundation on, which I guessed was to cover whatever imperfections she felt her skin had, and her lips were slightly wonky, with a scar under her nose. I admitted to myself that I was mostly enjoying the annoyance and surprise in her eyes rather than appreciating her as a potential fuck. I tend to avoid police officers. Mixing work and pleasure doesn't end well.

But now that I was closer to her, I could see that the dark hair was actually quite curly and required a number of hair clips to keep it all restrained. Even with the sheer number she had in, bits were still escaping. It was oddly fascinating; I wanted to know what it looked like when it wasn't restrained, and how it would curl around my fingers as I ran my hands through it...

No. Bad Nikolas. I really did not need extra trouble after the amount I'd already landed myself in that morning.

I waited for my police tail to get over her surprise that the man she'd seen walk into the bar was now behind her and inviting her for a drink, and settle for glaring at me. "Why would I want a drink with you?" she snapped at me.

"Saves you waiting outside for me to come out, no?" I pushed myself off the wall and gestured to the door. "White wine, I'd guess?"

I'd thoroughly unsettled her, but now my estimation went up. She gave me a glare and said, "Jack and coke, actually."

If she had enough spirit to recover from my little surprise and object to my choice of drink, then maybe she'd make a decent operative. I gave her a brief smile and opened the door for her. That got me a suspicious look, but she managed to stay in character enough to follow me to the bar. I ordered, we found a table, and took sips of our drinks in silence.

"So?" she asked as she put her drink down. Her tone was somewhere between suspicion and annoyance, and I took the opportunity to feel slightly smug. I'd definitely thrown her off-balance.

"Like I said, you may as well wait for me in here rather than pretend you're doing something outside."

"How did you know I was following you?"

"You need more practise," I told her. "Follow from ahead, and blend in. That office get-up is too obvious."

"It's my work outfit." A wash of colour flooded her face, even under the makeup. "I was on the desk."

I resisted the urge to apologise. "Did they seriously drag you off just to follow me?"

If anything, her face got redder. I felt like I should hand her a tissue.

"Wow," I commented. "Bastards. Well, I need to see someone, so you can have lunch here and I'll pick you up when I'm done, ok?"

"Stop patronising me." She was bright red, but the snap of backbone was there.

"You followed me," I pointed out.

She shut her mouth on whatever retort she'd been going to say, which I suspected was something to do with following orders or me being a troublemaker.

"Look, do you want lunch?" I asked, trying to turn on the charm a little. "Seriously, I need to see someone here, so if you're following me for the next hour you may as well get fed."

"I don't trust you," she muttered through the flush.

I resisted the urge to roll my eyes. I'd thought I was enough trouble to assign a tail to, but apparently, they just wanted to humiliate the trainee. "Look, I already sneaked up behind you once. I'm making your job easier here, ok? Sit here or don't, I don't care, but unless I pick you up when I leave you're not going to know when I've gone."

"I'm not that stupid!" she flared.

"I already snuck up behind you once." I stood and gave her my most charming smirk. "I'll see you in a bit, darlin'. Order at the bar. My tab."

***

I figured that as I was here—and somewhere that my police tail would be watched by eyes other than mine, just to make sure she didn't get into trouble—I may as well have a chat to the second big power who might want to help with giving Tanya a bloody nose.

"Who's the awkward one upstairs?" the Queen asked as soon as I'd sat down in the comfy chair on the other side of the desk. She was an older lady, but no less attractive for it; she knew what she wanted to look like, and didn't let wrinkles stand in the way of that. I actually liked her—I didn't trust her, of course, but I did like her.

"The Angels gave me a tail. I snuck up behind her and then invited her for a drink."

The woman opposite laughed, a genuine chuckle that I

didn't hear often. It was nice to see the mafia Queen relaxing enough to find something amusing. "We all have our diversions. So, what can I do for you?"

"How's progress on the Mardos take-down?"

The Queen eyed me. "You sleep with her, yet you don't like her?"

"I hate the bitch." The snap came out before I could stop it, and I knew I'd fucked up as soon as I said it.

"Sky," the Queen said thoughtfully after a moment. "I didn't think you were one to care, Nikolas, but it seems you've proved me wrong. Actually, I wanted to see you in the next few days about the Mardos, so you have good timing."

That was interesting. Could that have linked in at all to the police investigation? "Well, I'm still in for helping. I want that bitch taken down."

The Queen folded her hands. "She's running for Council."

"Oh, hell no."

"Hell, yes." Our eyes met over the table, and I saw the steely resolve in the mafia boss. "I don't like her business methods, but I will not tolerate her bribing her way into power."

"How long have we got?"

"A few months." The Queen drummed her fingers, and then said, "The first thing for you to do is get yourself out of there without alarming her in...say, the next two weeks. I don't want you in the line of fire, but I don't need her warned. Start that off and then come back to see me, and bring Sky. Got it?"

"Got it."

***

My tail was still in the bar when I came up the stairs from the basement—although to her, it was just the door to the toilets. The Queen would have told me if she'd done any snooping, and while I gave her points for sense, I also deducted them for lack of initiative. After all, if a dodgy contact takes you somewhere and tells you to stay put, doing it is just boring, right?

You might be able to tell how I got into quite as much trouble as I did when I was a teenager.

I stopped by the table, noting the empty plate that had probably contained a sandwich. "I don't know your name."

"I'm not going to tell you that." At least she had some sense.

"I'll just call you Sam, then. It's a good enough name for a dog."

"A dog?" The flush was roasting her face again.

"Well, you are a tail." I smirked. "Come on, then. Walkies?"

I was actually enjoying seeing her speechless, although I did feel a little bad. She'd been given a really crap duty, especially for a trainee. But them's the breaks.

I took her arm and escorted her out of the pub, keeping hold of it as she tried to pull away. "We came in together, we leave together. Now you walk in the other direction, cross the road at the lights and follow me on the other side. Not as obvious as fiddling with your phone for thirty seconds and then walking after me."

"I don't have a phone."

"Oh, shame. I was going to ask for your number." I leaned forward and gave her cheek a kiss before she could flinch away.

"I'm going to see a friend. You can follow for a bit. Heel, Sam!"

And I walked away before she could respond. I know, I'm such a bastard sometimes.

So, I'd got the first task on a list that I knew was going to grow as the Queen's operation rolled on. Somehow, get myself out of my position with Tanya Mardos. How the hell was I going to do that? She was a rich woman, head of a crime syndicate that very successfully masqueraded as legal, and she had me on speed dial—admittedly as a fuck-toy rather than anything more major, but I knew I could land myself in more hot water if I didn't play her right.

Maybe finding someone else for her to play with would work? What would Tanya Mardos like? I brought up a mental image of her. Big-breasted and blonde, with legs that went up to her armpits. A woman who knew what she liked—which was ordering her lovers around—and a definite exhibitionist. She got on with me because we'd had a discussion about dogs and then my obvious charms had won her over, or possibly she just liked a tall, sarcastic lover that she could boss around—not that I was sarcastic around her. I minded myself very carefully, partly because I'd got lots of lovely illegal access to her computer network due to my midnight booty calls, and partly because I hated the fucking bitch, which meant if I snapped, I'd probably land myself in a world of shit.

Anyway. If I could hook her up with someone else... someone who liked watching? A sub would suit her. It'd have to be a man, if only because I'd never heard a word breathed of a liking for women.

Hensch. He could hook me up, and that would solve

another of my list of problems.

It was only just gone midday, but I needed to head for the strip club.

***

I ambled along for a bit, keeping an eye out. My police tail was doing better now that I'd given her those pointers—I caught her, of course, but not as often and not as obviously. She'd need to get better at stopping when I stopped, or not, and she still stood out in that suit. It was made of cheap fabric, and the cut was awful. I appreciated that it was needed to cover the handcuffs or whatever, but really?

Luckily the strip club wasn't too far, so I didn't feel too bad about dragging Sam away from her desk. Did her boss actually hate her to dump her onto a tail with no experience, or did they seriously think I was that useless? I snorted. If I needed to lose her, I would, and she wouldn't even see my dust. But she might as well get some practise, I guessed. It wasn't like it was harming me for her to know where my favourite strip club was.

The man on the door was a very bored, spotty, middle-aged man—a candidate for a mid-life crisis if I ever saw one. I wondered absently what that would look like as I waited for him to call through to Hensch. He saw enough bodies, so it wouldn't be women...cars, maybe. A fast car. He'd need a bit more money than he got working on the door of a strip club, but he could win the lottery. There's hope for us all.

Out of the corner of my eye, I spotted Sam approaching. She had lingered long enough, and now knew she had to move —and pass me. She was being too obvious about not looking at us, and I saw the doorman clock her too. We shared a mutual glance.

"Trainee," I said.

"Ah." I caught the faint smile. "It shows."

"I gave her some pointers."

Sam headed past on the far side of the street, and I wondered what she'd do. Come in? Linger? I was going out the back way after this anyway, so I hoped she'd just go home.

Well, not really my problem.

When permission to enter arrived, I ambled my way through the strip club with a few afternoon patrons and a bored woman doing slow gyrations around a pole, and headed through a back door. I wanted the private club; the area where the dirty stuff went on. Through this private door, and you were allowed to touch as well as look—most of the time.

"Nikolas! Fortunate timing." Hensch was wearing his usual impeccable suit, and was an interesting contrast to the naked man tied spread-eagled on some sort of wooden contraption in the middle of the room. He didn't really suit the sophisticated brown leather chairs and grey walls, but I don't judge Hensch on his decorating tastes. "I'm just breaking him in. Care to join in?"

I eyed the naked man. His arms and legs were strapped down with leather to the wooden legs of what looked like a narrow-topped table, leaving his ass exposed and open at just the right height to be fucked. He was blindfolded, but I saw his head twitch where he was listening intently. He was slightly portly, his belly rolling into fat as it pressed against the horse, and his back had a streak of hair down the spine. He was also obviously excited to be where he was, if his cock was anything to go by.

"Not today, Hensch. Thanks for the offer." I didn't really want to say that the man did nothing to excite my own cock— I'm into both genders, but there's a time and a place, and I don't really like restraint. I'd much rather fuck someone who's free to grab what they want to, as long as it's done with passion. "I'm here to talk business."

Hensch wasn't at all offended by my refusal. "You don't mind if I work while we talk? Then you must have a seat and a drink."

Within five minutes, I was sitting in one of the comfortable high-backed armchairs with a cold beer, and Hensch was trailing a leather crop down the man's back. "So, to business." The bound man twitched as the crop ran over his buttocks, and then there was a swish-thwack of a strike.

A hurt groan escaped from the man and Hensch straightened, his attention snapping away from me before I could start to talk. I took a sip of my beer and watched as the suited man walked around to the front of the table, took the naked man's jaw in between his thumb and forefinger, and raised the blindfolded head.

"I have a business meeting, and I will not have interruptions. You will be silent." The bound man's skin was going white under Hensch's fingers, but Hensch's voice was surprisingly gentle. "Do you understand me?"

"Yes, Master."

Hensch strolled back along the table, and then there was another swish-thwack as the crop struck against the naked man's shoulder. He didn't groan, although I saw his jaw clench, and I winced in sympathy. That had to hurt.

"He needs it," Hensch said to me, seeing my expression. A

gesture of the crop drew my attention to the man's cock, hard and throbbing against the table. "But let us not talk of such trivial matters. You require a favour?"

I explained about Tanya and my job as her fuck-toy while Hensch walked around the table, entirely at ease in his smart suit as he teased and tormented his captive, trailing the crop across the man's naked skin and occasionally striking an unexpected blow. He asked a few questions about what we'd done, obviously trying to get an idea of Tanya's charms, and then produced a slim bottle of something from one jacket pocket. "Well," he said, drizzling the liquid onto the handle of his crop, "I believe you are correct that a sub would suit her. What is her physical type?"

"At the moment, me."

"This is possible." He turned and pushed the lubed-up crop handle against the naked man's buttocks. I heard the stifled groan and then the handle almost completely vanished, acting as a dildo. I wondered what it would be like to be fucked by that…particularly if someone was as wound up as the man on the table obviously was.

Then Hensch turned away, leaving the crop stuck up at a jaunty angle. The captive's cock was looking painfully hard, and I wondered how long Hensch was going to leave him there. "When do you need them by?" he asked me.

"As soon as possible."

"I will ask."

"Don't you just tell them?" I asked, puzzled. "They're subs. Aren't they meant to obey?"

"There is a degree of negotiation," Hensch said, smiling. "They obey when I ask them to do something they want to do.

Fucking Tanya Mardos was not in the contract, hey?"

I glanced at the twitching riding crop stuck in the man on the table, and shrugged. "That's fine. You'll call me?"

"Of course."

I drained the last of my beer and stood. "Then I'll let you finish up."

"As ever, you have precisely the right phrase."

I gave him a smirk, feeling a bit better. "All part of my charm."

*****

So, with that in progress, it was time to find out what the next step was to take down Tanya Mardos. The next day I was back at the Queen's headquarters—this time, with my girlfriend in tow.

"It's all about the legalities," the Queen said briskly. "I need something big enough to get her out of the game for at least this year, and ideally out permanently." She scowled. "Although that will be a long shot. I need to cripple her."

Sky and I were sitting opposite the older lady, who was drumming her fingers on the desk. I had a pint of coke, but Sky had opted for tea, which had been delivered by the Queen's chunk of security in a battered mug. It wasn't the prettiest waiter service I'd ever seen, but it did the job.

"The problem, really, is finding something to pin on her," the Queen continued as her security rumbled off to stand outside the door. "I could go old-fashioned and just shoot the bitch, but we don't need a reintroduction of that sort of fighting around here."

"You could go subtle?" Sky suggested.

"I think staying away from murder is a better idea," I put

in. I didn't need that tangling my job.

"I agree," the Queen said, and placed her hands together. "I think, however, we do have a potential lead. Do you remember the document that you were interested in when we first met, Nikolas?"

The one I'd paid for with an orgasm for the woman in front of me...and had got me involved with the woman next to me. "Yeah. Why?"

"Do you know what it was?"

I shrugged. "A list of names."

"A list of interested parties for bidding on an area of property in the city," Sky said. "I didn't get why it was relevant either."

The Queen smiled. "Up until a month ago, it wasn't. That was the point the bidding concluded. That bitch won."

"So...you want to see who she outbid?" I asked.

"Nearly. I want to see who she leaned on to withdraw." I think Sky's face reflected as much confusion as my own, and the Queen leaned back. "That was the original bid interest list on a key piece of property that's got a permit for redevelopment and legal clauses in the ownership deed. Whoever owns it will have a chance to influence the redevelopment of a large area around it, and in that bitch's case, do shoddy work, employ illegal workers, skim huge amounts of money off the top and launder even more as she does the building work. She's done it before." The Queen snorted. "Not that I object to any of those things, but I at least am not a bitch about it."

"So we already have the original list..." I said, trying to find the point.

"If we can get hold of the list of final bidders," the Queen said, "then we'll know who Tanya pressured, and they might be persuaded to assist with evidence."

"So you want to do this legally?" I asked. "Why not just suggest it to the Angels?"

"It's currently all speculation."

"They could get the bid document…"

"They'd need a warrant."

My brain was slowly catching up. "And so you'd have to persuade someone it was worth their time and effort to get a warrant?"

"Without tipping that bitch off. As soon as someone goes after the bidders she'll know what I'm up to."

And considering how much I felt the hold on the Angel's investigation stank, I wondered if she was right. I had one more try. "Surely the police are the better party to do that, though?"

The Queen sighed. "Nikolas. This is not my first show, and certainly not the first time I have tried to pin that bitch to the wall. She will make documents and people vanish. The law is not known for its subtle touch, and they aren't likely to be able to out-manoeuvre her."

"And they'd probably be far more interested in you than what you wanted them to do," Sky added to her employer.

I privately admitted that I agreed. After all, the Queen was the major reason I'd been sent on this investigation: Tanya Mardos hadn't even been in the running. "All right, so you want it private until you can dump a pile of evidence on someone's desk?"

"Oh, no. I want it private until I can get as many witnesses as possible, and then I will spread that muck everywhere. Even if she refutes it and somehow manages to silence everyone, the stink will cling. But up until then, I need it quiet, and then that bitch doesn't have time to set anything up to counter it all."

"Ok. So where do we come in?" I asked.

"I need the document, and then I need the witnesses."

"I assume it was an auction…" Sky mused. "Tremain again?"

"Indeed."

"I'll find someone to hack their files."

I followed that bit, at least. My computer-geek friend Benny was technically a white hat hacker, but when it came to legality, he'd proved himself agreeable to some slightly greyer shades. I blamed Sky.

"We should get Bear involved too," Sky said.

"The Jacks are expensive," the Queen said. "I admit their skills could be useful, particularly when it comes to breaking in, but their price is too high."

Sky's grin was the one that told me she was plotting something. "Bear's won't be. He hates Tanya."

The Queen didn't have to say anything. She simply gave Sky a look.

"Something recent," Sky said, answering the unasked question. "The price they quoted before when you asked for their help was valid, but…it was something personal." She made a face. "I couldn't get details."

"How do you know that?" I asked curiously.

"Jim told me." I suspect I gave her something similar to the Queen's look, as she rolled her eyes. "We get on fine now,

Nikolas. And it's what I *do*, remember?"

The Queen held up a hand to forestall the snarky remark about getting information not being all she did. "So Bear could be interested. Sky, find out his—no. Nikolas. Find out his price for assisting with smearing the Mardos bitch."

I hadn't spent much time with Bear since our fuck-date a few months back. We'd met occasionally in bars while on other business, and had a brief chat and a drink…

Well, I wasn't averse to getting back in contact. It had been a fun night, even if sex wasn't on the cards this time. "I'll ask him."

"Who else?" Sky asked.

"I have other contacts that might be useful, but I will talk to them," the Queen said briskly. "I didn't think the Jacks would help, but Bear would certainly be an asset. Find your hacker and get back to me."

Chapter Three

I contacted Bear as soon as we got to Benny's: Sky headed off to brief my grumpy friend on what he needed to hack, and I dumped myself out of the way in the tiny kitchen to send a message. Bear and I had been on a…well, I'd like to call it a date, but really it was an interview. Disguised as a date.

The hook-up afterwards had most definitely not been job-related, though.

"Got any gossip on Mardos? What's your price?"

My phone beeped just as I put it down, and I quickly picked it up again. Wait, already? He was fast.

"*Hi Nikolas. V.happy to talk. Price is dates with you.*"

My jaw nearly hit the floor. "Sky? Sky!"

She stuck her head round the door. "What?"

"Bear wants a date with me."

"Wh—Oh, for helping with Tanya?" A grin spread across

199

her face. "Seriously?"

"Yes!" I stared at the phone screen as if that would make the words change. "What the fuck?"

"You obviously made an impression."

"This is business, though!" I protested. "Why doesn't he want…I dunno, something out of the Queen?"

Sky rolled her eyes. "They're loaded already, Nikolas, and they've got people to do everything. Why would he not want a date?"

I glared at her ass as she headed back to talk to Benny, and then considered. I read the message again, and then sent, "Plural? How many?"

The reply came back mere seconds after I'd pressed send. "*Five.*"

Five? Hell no! Even if he was one sexy…I shook my head to clear my thoughts. Five dates, all ending like last time? I'd be stiff and sore for days. Not that it was a bad thing, but this was business. "One," I countered.

"*Three, final offer. Clear it with Sky.*"

"Sky!" I yelled.

"What?" she yelled back.

"He wants three dates and I have to clear it with you!"

"How many?"

"Three!"

"Sex?"

"Dunno." I texted, "What's involved in these dates?"

"*Food. Drink. Talk. Sex.*"

"Sex included," I yelled to Sky.

"Go for it."

That made me stand up and walk round to the living

room, where she was playing something fast-paced and bloody on the TV. "Would you have said no if it *didn't* include sex?"

"Well, yeah." She was still watching the TV, fingers twitching on the controller. "No point having a decent meal if you can't work off the calories afterwards."

"You are..." I wasn't sure if I should be exasperated or grateful. "Any other requirements?"

Sky huffed and paused the game, and then turned to me. "Nikolas, you like him. He likes you. Go and fuck him, and it puts us one step closer to fucking up Tanya for good."

"You're not...bothered?"

"We've been through this, baby." She means 'idiot' when she calls me that, but she did stand up and come to hug me. "I want you to be happy. I love having sex with you, and I love spending time with you. But I want you to be able to fuck whoever else you want. I know you love me, and I don't take that for granted. But sex is just fun. Go do it."

I was laughing, and leaned down to kiss her. "Yes, ma'am."

There was a snort from behind us: Benny doesn't do emotions, particularly not when they involved bodily fluids. "I've started the hack."

Before we could say anything, he turned and headed back towards his room. Sky and I looked at each other, and shrugged. He'd come out when he'd got what we needed.

***

Unfortunately, two hours later, that wasn't the result.

I looked up from having my ass thoroughly kicked by Sky —metaphorically—to see Benny standing in the doorway.

"It's blank."

"What?"

"The file's blank."

We followed him through to his room. He'd got into the Tremain systems, and I could see the file structures. Right file. Right date. The name looked right, too; that was the property.

But the document was blank.

"So they didn't record the data?" Sky asked.

"Someone wiped it…" I leaned over. "Benny, can you get anything on the last date it was changed?"

"Hmm." He tapped a few commands, and a box popped up. "Five days ago. Admin."

"Fuck."

"Not really," Benny said. "The staff all have individual logins."

It took a moment for that to click. "So it was someone outside the system?"

"Yeah."

"It was deliberately wiped," I growled. "Can you get any information on who…"

"That doesn't help us," Sky interrupted. "We need what was on that document. Whoever wiped it probably didn't bother backing up a copy."

I turned to look at her. "Backups."

"Yeah? They would have deleted those, surely…"

"They've got an offsite backup," Benny said, "but it updates every ten days. It'll take me a bit of time to get in there; they're a lot more secure, but they should have—"

"You try that," I told Benny, and turned to Sky again. "Tremain's do paper backups."

"What?"

"I investigated before the theft. It was easier to get the

digital one, but with you and Bear helping…"

"Your lockpicking skills not up to much?" Sky asked, grinning at me.

"They're shit," I admitted. "I'm sure there's got to be a better way than breaking in, anyway."

"All right." Sky cracked her knuckles. "Benny, get hacking. I'll get investigating."

"What do you want me to do?" I asked.

"Get yourself out of Tanya's range before this blows."

***

Actually, it wasn't Tanya Mardos that was immediately worrying me. Bear had booked me in for the next evening, and I admit I spent some of the day worrying about what to wear.

"Whatever you want," was Sky's unhelpful suggestion when I came back for lunch. "He'll just take it off you again."

"That really doesn't help," I grumbled, and went back to eating a sandwich with one hand and checking out something I'd got Benny to steal for me with the other.

Sky twitched the sheet of paper out of my fingers. "Classified?"

"Police eyes only," I told her as I snatched it back.

"Why are you looking at organisational charts?"

"Because I want to know who has the authority to put an investigation on hold."

"Did you have Sam following you again?"

"Not that I saw, but I doubt she knows where to find me." I snorted. "The bar or the strip club, and I didn't go to either today."

"She'd have your address, though."

"I doubt she's got the skills for a stake-out."

Sky was giving me a stare. "You did check this morning, right?"

"Of course I did." I'd spent ten minutes standing unobtrusively near the window, checking out the likely hiding spots before leaving. "I just find it incredibly suspicious that I ask about Tanya, get told it's on hold when nothing else is, and then get a tail…"

"The tail makes no sense, though. They know where Tanya lives."

"But maybe not where I meet her?" I shrugged. "She's not a good tail. Look, I'm just indulging my paranoia."

Sky peered over my shoulder. "So, likely suspects?"

"Four." I tapped the names. "Anyone else would likely not obeyed. I'll focus on them first."

"Are you going to do some digging for blackmail?"

"You bet I am." I folded the chart and headed off to give it back to Benny. He'd destroy it. "And find out who exactly has been fucking Tanya Mardos on the sly."

"What time's your date?" Sky called after me.

"8pm," I admitted. "He's cooking."

"Oh?" Sky had a wicked grin. "Have fun."

***

When I got to the tower block, it was just before 8pm. I'd worried about my clothes, then about what to take—I'd settled on beer this time. And then I'd just worried.

Bear was a member of the Jacks: jack-of-all-trades, safecrackers and hackers and bodyguards. Last time had been a…test of my skills, so to speak, set up by one of his fellow Jacks. Bear hadn't known he was the target, and I wasn't intending to enlighten him.

But the sex had been great. I wondered if that was why he'd asked for dates as a price for his help this time…

The buzzer went, and I said, "It's Nikolas," to the box.

"*Come on up.*"

The door was open when I got out of the lift, and I gave a cursory knock. I admit I was a little on edge, not sure what to expect…

Low lighting. Fantastic smells. And Bear, bearded and smiling, walking towards me…

Holy fuck.

He was wearing an apron. Just an apron.

It covered most of his torso, and wasn't too tight, but…

I swallowed, and held out the beer. "I certainly wasn't expecting this."

"Nice to see you too," Bear said, laughing, and reached past me to close the door. I glanced down, and his back was bare; the dangling apron strings were swaying across his ass, and his shoulder brushed past mine. "Come on in and have a seat. I'm just finishing up."

I took the indicated chair at the bar that formed the edge of the kitchen, and appreciated the set-up. I could see the chef in all his glory, and the bar would hide my erection—and he could serve up appetisers without leaving the confines of his cooking space, as he immediately proved.

"Edamame beans," he said, putting another small bowl down next to the one filled with some sort of sauce. "Dip them in that, suck 'em out."

"You're going to have to demonstrate."

He took one of the beans out of the bowl, dipped it whole into the brown sauce, and then put it into his mouth. I watched as he tugged it back out, obviously popping the beans out of the shell and straight onto his tongue. I wanted him to do that with my cock…

"Uh. Right." I took a bean. "I'll try it."

I ate the beans and watched as Bear went back to prepping. There was obviously something in the oven, and he was stirring a pan as well as doing something with a frying pan. A couple of plates to one side had piles of things on.

"So," Bear said, still stirring his pan. "What exactly is this job?"

"You agreed to this without knowing the details?" I gave him a skeptical look.

"I like to hear it from the people involved."

I was watching him as he cooked, admiring the way his ass moved. His back was covered in the same thick hair as his torso, but for whatever reason, the hair on his ass was thinner. I liked the way it moved with the muscles underneath.

"Nikolas?"

"Oh, yeah." I pulled my mind back to business. "The Queen's trying to get her ducks in a row to take out Tanya legally. She bought a property off Tremain's, and we've got the original list of interested bidders. If we can get the list of actual bidders, we can work out who Tanya scared off, and hopefully get them to testify."

"That sounds awfully complex."

"You offer a simpler solution." I'd spent a while thinking about it in between worrying. If Tanya had somehow been involved in stopping the police investigation, it meant that she did have tendrils everywhere. The Queen was right that we'd need to keep it private—or quiet, at least. And the police were not known for quiet, as Sam had proved. So, hack the files and talk to everyone we could?

Bear shrugged. "Well, I've actually got a different suggestion. I've got some decent gossip, and I'm happy to have a chat to the Queen about it…as long as you pay my price."

"If it's all going to be this good, count me in." He'd just put a plate of small, sticky balls of what looked like rice in front of me. "Dare I ask?"

"Just try one." Bear put one to my lips, and I opened my mouth, wanting to lick his fingers as he gently pushed the ball in. I got a mouthful of squishy rice with a spicy centre, and he winked at me, taking one for himself. "Next."

That was a plate of more rice, layered with… "Seaweed?"

"And vegetables." He dipped the rectangle into the brown sauce before raising it to my lips, and a trickle of the sauce ran down his finger. I captured his hand as I bit into the food, and followed the trail down his finger with my tongue, vinegar and salt contrasting with the flavours in my mouth.

Bear's cheeks were pink under the beard; whether from the heat of the stove or me, I wasn't sure. And then his eyes widened. "Whoops!"

I watched as he dived back to the stove and rescued whatever the next thing was. Something came out of the oven —crispy squares with sesame seeds on top—and then another dish, tiny puffs of sweet dough with spicy filling; then strips of fried meat, and another rolled seaweed-and-rice concoction. A taster morsel from every dish was slipped between my lips by Bear before he left the plate in front of me, and my cock was rock-hard in my trousers as I watched him move around the kitchen, muscles sliding under his skin as he stirred and bent.

"How are you liking it all?" he asked.

"Very much. Oh, you mean the food?"

He laughed, and brought another plate over. "You didn't expect this, then?"

"I had no idea you were so skilled."

"Dessert's a bit more pedestrian, I'm afraid. You like chocolate?"

"Yeah?"

"Excellent."

Bear came round to sit at the end of the bar and together we finished off the dishes as he told me what they contained. Food isn't usually my thing—as long as it tastes ok, I'm good —but boy do I like watching someone talk about whatever they're interested in. Particularly if they're doing it while only wearing an apron.

Bear fed me the final morsel, and then stacked the plates. "So, dessert?"

"Sure."

"Clothes off."

I blinked. "What?"

"I need a serving platter. Clothes off."

He was taking the empty plates off the bar and over to the sink, and I really had to obey the chef in his own kitchen, didn't I? I began to undo my shirt as Bear found a clean pan and ingredients in a cupboard, and began to mix something in a bowl. He really did have a nice ass...

He glanced back over his shoulder at me and nodded appreciatively. "Sit up on the bar."

I looked down at the surface as I pulled my socks off. It seemed fairly sturdy, and I realised that Bear had cleared the top. "You sure?"

"It'll be fine." Bear wasn't looking at me, intent on whatever he was doing at the stove.

I took my trousers off, and I had to admit that my erection had subsided a bit. Sure, he was sexy, but...what was about to happen? I hopped myself up onto the worktop, sitting with my legs dangling, watching the chef at work.

Bear turned, and found me opposite him. "Oh, nice," he said, and lifted a finger to my lips. "I could use a clean-up..."

Chocolate. I greedily licked his finger, feeling my cock stir.

Bear pulled his hand away, laughing. "Why don't you lie down? I'll bring more over."

I sprawled myself sideways on the bar with my head propped on one hand, thanking whichever designer had made it wide enough to actually fit a grown man's ass on. Or maybe Bear had designed it that way? How often did he have naked men on it?

I asked him as he came back over with a plate containing strawberries, and he gave me an amused look. "You obviously missed the part where I said I hadn't had sex for a while. You're the first. It just sounded like a fun idea, and it's the right height..." He trailed off.

"Do I look like I'm not enjoying it?" I asked him, gesturing to my cock with one hand and stealing a strawberry with the other.

"No, you're definitely...up for it." Bear took the strawberry out of my hand and pushed it slowly between my lips. I definitely wanted his cock there as he slid it out again, our eyes meeting, and then my mouth was filled with the sweet, sharp taste.

"Hold it there," Bear said, and stepped across the kitchen. A moment later he was back with a bowl filled with something…chocolate.

I sucked his finger, running my tongue around and down, pulling it in and tasting the chocolate against the strawberry already on my tongue. And then Bear got another fingerful, but instead of sliding it between my lips, he swirled it around my nipple. It was warm and soft, smooth against my skin.

"Fuck…" I couldn't help the moan as his tongue ran down my chest and his lips fastened on the chocolate, sucking at my nipple. "Oh, fuck."

"On your back," Bear said, and I shifted myself so that the worktop was cool underneath me, my shoulders against the hard surface. There was the sudden warmth of chocolate against the other nipple, his fingers running down my stomach, and Bear's beard tickled my skin and his mouth was over my nipple, teeth gently biting until his tongue trailed after his fingers. A strawberry felt rough against my mouth, turning smooth and sweet when I bit into it, as his tongue and lips trailed over my shoulder and down to my hip. I wanted him to touch my cock, hard and pulsing with the build-up, and he slowly trailed chocolate and tongue around the base, across my thighs and balls as I spread my legs and gasped with the mix of sensation.

When he did finally touch my cock, I couldn't help the groan, so desperate for release—but it was warm, smooth, a sensation like nothing else, and then the warmth of his mouth and lips followed, licking the chocolate off, surrounding me and sucking up and down until every last drop of sweetness had been devoured.

"Salt and chocolate, it works," Bear said, and ran another trail of chocolate down my shaft, into my balls, the warmth almost painful against the cold he'd left behind from his mouth. I was bucking upwards, needing his mouth on me again, desperately ready to come. But he started from my balls, licking and teasing, and then slid upwards as he followed the trail of chocolate. Something pushed against my lips and I opened my mouth to find chocolate, another strawberry sliding in, and then as I swallowed I had Bear's lips and tongue against mine as he kissed me.

"You want to finish?" he asked.

"Yes." I pushed myself up onto my elbows. My body was surprisingly clean, with just occasional smears of chocolate or strawberry across my skin. My cock was hard and pulsing. "I want to watch."

Bear dipped a finger in the bowl of chocolate and brought it to my lips, and I kept eye contact as I sucked it, letting him push in and out, fucking my mouth. He was hard too, tenting the apron. Another fingerful of chocolate trailed downwards and I watched as he outlined my nipples again, following the trail with his tongue, down towards my cock. He smeared the chocolate all over my shaft, and then his mouth followed, surrounding and sucking, and I came—shuddering and swearing, salt and sweetness, my hands grasping at nothing and my head spinning, my mouth full of chocolate and his full of cum.

"Fuck," I said as he swallowed and then lifted his head from my cock. "Fuck."

"Well, yes." Bear nabbed a finger of the chocolate and sucked it off his own fingers.

"I want a go," I said, and swung my legs off the bar.

"I won't last long," Bear warned.

And he didn't. I didn't bother putting him on the bar, or anything fancy—I pushed his apron up, swirled a fingerful of chocolate on the tip of his cock, and took him into my mouth with his ass against the counter and his hands gripping my shoulders. Four strokes later he was coming, filling my mouth with salt and gasping out my name from above.

"Well," he said, wiping one hand across his forehead as I withdrew and stood. "Good dinner?"

"Unusual." I looked around. The kitchen had its fair share of pans, dirty plates and general chaos that comes from cooking—and the bar had managed to get a nice mix of sweat, chocolate and juice. "I'll help you wash up."

"Oh, really?" Bear said, eyeing my body. "Well, the shower's this way."

"Dishes first?" I suggested, smiling. "Then…I could handle a shower."

Chapter Four

So Bear was in for whatever we needed him for—not that I really had any idea. I let the Queen know we had another conspirator, and went back to plotting. Sky was running round talking to people, and Benny was still hacking—or playing Halo, I wasn't quite sure which. Certainly Halo seemed to be on his screen more than the moving wall of text, but it's often hard to tell with Benny. I left them to it, anyway.

It was two days later when I got a message from Hensch. He'd found someone for Tanya, and it would repay the favour that he owed me. I debated if that was a fair price, but then decided it probably was. If it would get me out of Tanya's clutches but still keep me in her good books, that sounded fair…

But I'd need to check with the woman herself. Well, that wasn't too difficult, as I was booked in with her for that evening. One naked Tanya and two screaming orgasms later, I took the glass of champagne that she offered me and said, "I've got a proposal for you."

"Oh?"

"I've got a friend who really likes watching, and I think you'd like him. I want you to meet him."

"You don't have time for me?"

"I always have time, but you need more than I can give. If you had two of us…"

She cast an eye over my body and leaned back in the chair. "I like you, but this is true. What's the price?"

She's not stupid, so this was the hard bit. "He belongs to Hensch."

Tanya pursed her lips. "A rental?"

"That I'll pay for."

She's not one to pass up a bargain, but she pouted. "Am I really too much?"

"Tanya, you have twice the drive I do, and you deserve to have it all." I smiled at her. "I still want to play, though. This is in addition to me." I wanted to stay in her good books, despite the Queen's order to get out. The contact was useful, and if I offered a complete replacement, I didn't know if I'd get in again.

She smiled, looking like a lioness about to eat a nice meal. "You bring him here and I'll try."

***

The next day was filled with small chores and conversations, and ended, not unsurprisingly, at the strip club. Hensch had messaged me to say that I could come to check the potential sub out before I took him to Tanya, so after a long, boring meal with a contact that got me one piece of useless information, I headed over. I was absently wondering about my police tail as I took a winding route: I hadn't spotted Sam recently, but then if she didn't have the obvious start of me at the police HQ, would she ever find me? She'd be likely to stake out the few places she now knew, which were…well, the Queen's pub, and the strip club. And the Angels knew where I lived. I'd have to start checking for an unsubtle shadow every time I left.

I thought about her hair again, unruly curls, and then dragged my mind back to business as Sky's bright blue hair intruded and my cock started getting interested. I'd see her later.

The bouncer on the door was a different one, although he was just as much a candidate for a mid-life crisis—this would be an affair, I decided. He seemed to be taking more care of his muscles than most. I was let in, and found the club more lively than on my previous visit. There was a small band at the far end of the space, playing some quite decent music. Most of the poles were occupied by varying amounts of flesh, and everyone present seemed to be pretty happy.

And over by the far wall, leaning against a tasteful mural, was someone I recognised. She was wearing tight jeans and a black top that revealed a slash of cleavage, and looked pretty uncomfortable as she watched the room. Well, well…and just when I'd been wondering where she'd gotten to. Was she here on police business, or was this a side to my tail that I hadn't guessed?

She only clocked me when I was a meter away, and hadn't decided whether to run or stay by the time I stopped next to her. I gave her a pleasant smile. "Fancy seeing you here. Business or pleasure?"

She managed a glare. "What are you doing here?"

"I'm here on business," I said. "So, I'm guessing this is pleasure."

"Um." She was starting to flush bright red again, and I found I quite enjoyed the tell. She wouldn't be able to lie if she wanted to. It was rather adorable.

"Well?" I prompted.

She was still flushing, obviously reluctant to say anything; eyes darting, looking for a way out.

And so I turned up the menace factor. I took a step in front of her and leaned forward, resting an arm against the wall on one side of her. The other side was free, so she could leave, but I was far closer than I'd normally be, and I was glaring down at her.

"What are you doing here, Sam?" I murmured, dropping my voice into a quiet, throaty growl.

Her eyes were about level with my chin, and I got a good look at the dark curls of hair escaping in unruly tangles. I found myself wondering again what it would be like to wind my hands through them.

She managed to move her head, lifting her chin up. "You...won't..."

"I won't tell, Sam. I'm not a blackmailer." My tone managed to convey the contempt I felt, even though I'd tried to keep the statement neutral. "I don't judge other people on their kinks."

I saw her shoulders sag, the breath leaving her chest. "Oh."

"I have a girlfriend, and she doesn't mind me playing, but

I'd need to ask first." I gave her a moment, and then said, "You looked up my record. I never saw you here, Sam. So tell me what you're doing here."

Sam's voice was almost too quiet to hear under the chatter filling the bar, and I leaned my head down towards her. "I...I liked it. I wanted to find someone...I didn't think anyone would recognise me."

"Liked what?" My growl wound around her red cheeks, and I watched as her fingers wove themselves into each other.

"You...told me..."

"You liked me telling you what do to?" My voice was dropping further, down into a husky whisper. I was close to her now; not quite touching, but close enough that we would only needed a gentle movement to be pressed against each other. "Telling you that you're a dog, following me around?"

She was shaking, her eyes fastened on my chest, the flush lighting her cheeks.

"What if I called you the bitch you are?" My lips were close to her ear now, my cheek almost against her hair. "Told you to do exactly what I said, like a good puppy, so eager to please?" I could see her lips, moving faintly as she sucked in quick breaths. "Such a well-trained, obedient little dog. How about I find you a temporary owner, someone a bit safer than the bastards you'll find here. Now, you're going to be a good puppy and you're going to stay by me while we find him, ok?"

I drew back a little, lifted my free hand and put it under her chin, raising her eyes to mine. She still wasn't sure, and I saw the humiliation and desire warring in her face.

But she nodded.

***

We headed for the second door—this time with another, discreet, bouncer who gave me a small nod as Sam and I approached. A corridor led to another room, mostly empty; a bar filled up most of the far end, with a mixture of assorted furniture, booths, poles and floor cushions taking up the rest, scattered with the occasional chatting pairs. I found Hensch at the nearest end, sitting on a sofa with a couple of chairs around, chatting to a man wearing a catsuit and another in what looked like a designer dress. He raised his drink when he saw me. "Nikolas! What brings you here?"

"I need a favour."

The suited man rose and we moved off from the chairs a little to let them have their conversation. There was private drinks service in this area, and I managed not to ogle the skinny young man wearing a fox tail and not much else who came by with a tray. I noticed Sam's eyes following him too, and Hensch grinned at me. "So? I just repaid one, you want to owe me now?"

"You'll like this one."

He looked round my shoulder at Sam, who was hovering nervously behind me. "To do with her?"

I lowered my voice. "She's got a yearning for puppy play but doesn't know the ropes."

"You want me to break her in?"

"I want her to watch for the time being. Tell her to sit somewhere, tell her to get herself off if she wants to, but don't involve her. Just let her see."

He gave me a long look. "You know I don't usually do that."

"You know that Pol loves watchers."

"How did you know I had Pol tonight?" Both eyebrows shot up.

I grinned. "I talk to people. You'll look after her, ok? No playing. She's really new to the scene, Hensh."

His expression softened, just for a moment. "Yeah. I'll let her watch, and we'll see if she wants to come back. Cute little thing."

"She's obedient, too," I said in a slightly louder voice, and half-turned to tug Sam forward by her shoulder. "Sam, this is Hensh. He'll show you what he does with his pets. If you like it, you can come back. If you don't, then neither of us ever saw you here. Ok?"

She was shaking again, and her face was still fiery red. But she nodded.

I gave her shoulder a squeeze and nodded to Hensh, who beckoned to the fox-tail. A few murmured words and Sam was heading off towards the door in the far wall, which I knew contained the multitude of dressing-rooms and most likely Pol. Sam would be in good hands.

Hensch turned back to me. "Are you here for the evening?"

"I might as well be." I shrugged. "I'm here to see your sub for Tanya."

"Ah, of course. Well, have a seat and a drink. Did you bring her?" He motioned towards to door that Sam had disappeared behind.

I snorted as I took one end of the sofa. "No, she was in the strip club."

"She's a pretty little puppy."

"Not my type, Hensch. I don't mix work and play."

He raised an eyebrow, accepted the hint, and nodded. "You are my guest here, so you can play if you want. You know the rules, of course?"

I nodded. "I'm not a complete philistine, Hensh. Look unless you're allowed to touch, and don't get in the way of someone else's fun."

He grinned at me. "I'll tell you when your sub is ready to view."

He returned to his conversation with the designer dress as the fox-tail returned and brought me a drink, and then I was distracted by a woman wearing sparkles and...well, mostly sparkles. Lots of them. It was quite impressive, but I did wonder how she'd managed to get them to stick on. She came and sat down with me, and we had a good conversation about that while the room filled up.

The secret's eyelash glue, apparently, although it does smell like butt. That's a direct quote. I didn't ask for a sniff.

By the time I had extracted myself from the strange world of tassles and sequins, the room had more people in with varying accessories, but all mostly naked. I spotted several tails, some masks, a lot of leather, handcuffs, and one bald, broad-shouldered man in only heels and a collar, being led around by a petite woman in a leather pencil skirt. In this room, being dressed felt like the most unusual thing. Hensch leaned over and tapped my arm. "The demonstration is ready, if you would like?"

I nodded and followed him. I spotted a fully-clothed Sam a little way in; she was sitting on a low chair with a puppy's head on her knee, chatting to Pol and patting the dog's head. It was only when I got a step further that I realised why her cheeks were so red; someone was fucking the puppy at the other end. Well, Sam was definitely in for an education, and Pol was obviously looking after her. I left them to it.

I understood what Hensch meant by a demonstration when we had navigated enough bodies to get closer to the bar. There was a high-backed chair, and a woman sitting in it; roundly curved, with jet-black hair and a mass of pubic curls that seemed to spring from nowhere. She was entirely naked, and seemed completely unbothered by the appearance of two clothed men.

"Here," Hensch said, gesturing down. I'd assumed that the woman had her feet on a dark leather footstool, but at a closer look, it was a man.

"Could I, uh, have a look at him?" I asked.

"Ma'am, if you would?" Hensch asked the woman in the chair, who nodded and graciously removed her feet.

"Prince, this man wants to look at you," she told the footstool, poking him with one toe. "Stand."

I felt a bit off-balance, but the man stood. Tall, enough muscle to make Tanya happy…and a mop of black hair that she'd be able to grasp. So far, so good.

"Mistress Ren here is his current dom," Hensch said. "She can answer any questions."

I breathed a sigh of relief that he'd anticipated my sudden worry, and turned to the woman in the chair. "What's he good at?"

"Oral," the woman said, "and fucking."

"I need someone who can…" I tried to think of a way to phrase it. "She's an exhibitionist. I need someone with some initiative."

The woman's face split into a smile. "He'll be fine. He obeys me, but he'll do you proud. Do you want a demonstration?"

That was what I'd been dragged over here for so I couldn't really disappoint them. I nodded.

Actually, oral when someone else is doing it isn't that interesting. All I could really see was the man's head moving as he buried his face into the thick, dark curls, and so I watched the woman instead. She had such an intent look that I wondered if she was taking notes, possibly for points later. How do you score an orgasm?

Ok, I'm being cynical. It was hot. There's something about orgasms, just the wild abandon that they force on everyone, that's sexy as hell. However detached you want to be, the flush starts and muscles shake, legs tremble, and when her fingers tightened on the arms of the chair and her breathing quickened, my cock was already rising. I watched that glorious woman scream out swear words forced up through her body by the rising wave of pleasure, and felt my own cock twitch with desire.

Yeah, it was hot.

I had regained most of my composure by the time the man withdrew his damp, sweaty face, although I did suspect that Hensch next to me was smirking slightly. "He's good, then," I said.

"Adequate."

He'd brought her to orgasm in less than ten minutes. I called that a win. "All right, I'll give him a try. So what's the deal?"

"We'll discuss," Hensch said, and beckoned to the sub as

he took my arm to lead me back to the sofas. "Another drink, I think."

***

An hour later, I'd got the ground rules, a mild alcoholic glow, and the number for the local taxi firm. Tanya was free, and considering I had got fairly wound up inside the club—surprising myself, but there you go—I was happy to have an outlet.

Prince was now sitting next to me, wearing slacks and a t-shirt, and looking surprisingly chilled.

"So, what made you take this on?" I asked. We'd had a conversation about how our relationship was going to work: Prince and I had settled on rough equals for anything outside the bedroom, and I refused to do any commanding inside it. That was Tanya's problem. However, if she wanted me to fuck him, I wouldn't be saying no.

"It should be fun," Prince said cheerfully. "She sounds like a blast."

"With a high sex drive."

"Suits me."

"So, uh…" I suspected that Prince knew what I was going to ask, but he politely waited for me to finish the question. "How did you get into this lifestyle?"

"Pure accident. Group of friends brought me down to the club, spotted someone going in with rather more leather than I'd normally associate with strippers, asked the bouncer and got let in. Got hooked. Haven't looked back." He had an engaging smile. "How about you?"

"Met Hensch, found out what he did. I don't…"

"Play," Prince supplied.

"Yeah. I just came to see if you'd solve a problem for me, really."

"Friction burn?" Prince grinned broadly.

"Too right."

Tanya was waiting for us when we stepped into her living room, fully clothed and with the lights on. I wondered if she'd just had a business meeting. "Nikolas, how delightful!"

"Tanya, this is Prince," I said. "Your new toy."

"For your pleasure, ma'am, if you'd like me," Prince said, somewhere between demure and sexy. I noticed his voice had dropped into lower register.

"Oh, yes." Tanya was prowling around the man, and I'd seen nicer smiles on a tiger. "I like. What's your favourite position?"

"I like watching, ma'am," Prince said with a smile. "Wherever I can see you best."

"Oh, I like him." It was a definite purr. "Nikolas, you have time, yes?"

"For you, always."

"Then we will test him." This room had a wide desk with chairs in front and behind, and Tanya waved a hand to the chair in front of the desk. "You sit. Nikolas, I want to be fucked. Hard."

"Yes, ma'am."

Prince took the seat as instructed, and I dug in the drawer for a condom as Tanya waited, eyeing Prince thoughtfully with that smile still on her lips. I wondered what she was imagining doing to him...probably something to do with that thick, dark hair. Her hands entwined in it, and his mouth against her cunt, most likely. Knees bent, head thrown back, grinding her pussy against his lips and tongue as he made her scream.

I opened my jeans, unrolled the condom onto my cock, and with one swift movement pressed Tanya's shoulders down until her body was against the desk, breasts pressed hard against the surface, ass curving out to meet me in her tight skirt.

"You wanted hard." I leant down to speak into her ear as my hand slid under her hemline and pushed the fabric up. "And fast. And fierce. With him watching, taking in every moment of your beauty."

I'd learned that she didn't like the traditional scenarios of punishment, or submission—not for Tanya Mardos, oh no! She was still in control, even when she was being bent over a desk and fucked. One reason why I did not want her anywhere near politics; her views on diplomacy would likely tend towards the bullying.

Her skirt was up around her waist, and the flimsy fabric of her underwear was down around her ankles. I suspected that Prince was getting a very good view of her breasts, pushing out of her shirt, but I had more important things to play with.

Hard, and fast.

I thrust into her, tugging her thighs apart and holding them there, keeping her forced against the desk as I pulled out and thrust in again. She moaned and I saw her hands go out, gripping the desk, keeping her spread-eagled on the surface. "Yes, oh yes, yes, harder, yes…"

"I want to see your breasts," Prince said from the other side of the desk, his eyes fixed on Tanya. "May I?"

She gave a yes that was lost in a moan as I pushed in again, and then I gripped her hips and stayed in, my fingers digging in to her flesh as she pushed her shoulders up, letting Prince's fingers get to her shirt. He pulled it open, tugged un-gently at the bra, and then I was thrusting again and Tanya's groan of approval told me that her nipples had met the coldness of the desk, rubbing and pulling along the surface.

"You," she gasped at Prince. "Your cock. In my mouth."

That was a new one to me, but then I'd never been with her when she'd had two men to play with. I kept up my rhythm, thudding my hips against her ass as Prince opened his fly and rolled on a condom. He was obviously turned on, and loving the sight of Tanya—and, I suspected, the orders.

She let go of the desk as he stepped in front of her, grabbed his hips and pulled him to her, slurping and gagging as my next thrust pushed her too far. It took us a moment to get a rhythm, but soon her muffled groans told me that we were doing something right, and I started to quicken my pace. She was getting there, if the tension around my cock was right.

Prince met my eyes for a brief moment, something blissful in his; the same kind of expression Sky got when I told her to hold on to the bedframe and not let go, or spanked her until she was rock-hard and desperate to come. And then his eyes went back to Tanya, her mouth full of his cock and her cunt full of mine, as happy as someone with a high sex drive and two men to play with can be.

It didn't take long before she was screaming and her muscles tightened, her legs coming around me to hold me in as her cunt spasmed around my cock. It felt good, and I had to push the feeling away.

Prince stepped away, his wet cock still hard, and I

withdrew. Tanya pushed herself back off the desk, skirt around her waist and shirt half-undone, her breasts red and nipples hard where they'd been rubbing against the desk. I'll say this for the woman, she has a lot of self-confidence. She didn't even worry about what she looked like—which, incidentally, was mussed, flushed, and hot as hell.

"I like." She favoured Prince with another smile, and then turned it on me. "So far, he is a good choice."

I smiled back. "You've only had one orgasm, ma'am. Can we assist you with another?"

She considered it. "I have time."

It only took half a minute for the next scene to play out; Tanya's clothing on the floor, and Tanya herself sprawled naked in her desk chair; Prince kneeling on the floor half-under the desk, his erection still rock-hard out of his fly; and me, ass on the desk and a leg either side of Prince, making steamy eye contact with the naked woman in front of me.

"You watch," Tanya purred, and I settled my ass more comfortably as she did what I'm sure every lover did to Prince; wound her fingers into his hair, and brought his mouth to her still-wet cunt.

Prince went to work happily, hands grasping Tanya's buttocks. She lifted her legs and put one foot either side of me on the desk, tipping her head back and letting her fingers stroke through Prince's hair, the picture of indolence and relaxation. The dark head was moving slowly as he licked and teased, and I could see a flush rising across Tanya's breasts.

She tipped her head forward and met my eyes again as her breathing quickened. "Nikolas. I am a display for you. You love watching."

"I do." I gave her the sardonic smile that she took as pleasure.

"I am better than those porn women. I am real." It was like a challenge—I hadn't told her that my personal fantasy came with bright blue hair and a cock. "Come on me."

Shit.

I couldn't really disobey a direct command, so I pushed myself a little more upright and began stroking. I'd made myself a deal, back when I first started fucking Tanya Mardos, that I wouldn't come for her. I'd do most things she asked—within my own limits—but my orgasm wasn't something she'd have.

And even though the naked, blonde, panting woman in front of me was sexy, and did turn me on, I couldn't do it. My hand felt good, but it just wasn't building. Wasn't there. I didn't want to finish in front of this bitch.

Sky. I loved the way her shoulders slimmed down into her chest and waist, the bones of her hips, the way her cock reared out of that smooth stomach. I loved her ankles, and trailing my tongue up the backs of her knees and thighs, and the way my teeth bit into her ass, making her yelp and grind against me as I caught her hips and slid one hand around to grasp her cock, pinning her, moaning—

I wasn't even seeing the woman in the chair as she screamed out her pleasure and my warm cum spattered across her stomach. It was only a moment later, as the last of my pleasure pulsed out, that I came back to the room and the woman in front of me.

Prince was drawing out the last of Tanya's orgasm, and then withdrew a little as she lifted her head up and removed her hand from his hair. His face was coated, shiny with her fluids.

"Yes." She lifted her legs down and leaned forward, ignoring the spatter of fluid on her stomach. "I like you. Nikolas, you bring him again."

"He's yours to call on, ma'am," I said, trying not to show I was panting. I wouldn't let her see my pleasure, either. For Tanya Mardos, I was a toy. That was it.

"Excellent." The tiger's purr came back out, and then she waved a hand. "I will shower. You can go."

I noticed that I'd managed to get cum over Prince's shirt as he stood, but that's one of the hazards of fully-clothed sex, I guess. He was looking a little spaced out, with a funny little happy smile on his lips, so I tucked my cock away, made sure his was back in his trousers, and led him out.

Much as I liked the guy, I'd let him deal with his sexual tension on his own.

Chapter Five

It was 2am before I got home after dropping off Prince. I left my mobile number with him and instructions to be on call, usually anytime from 10pm. Evenings seemed to be when Tanya Mardos was most horny. I wasn't sure if she'd call him without me, or even if she'd call him at all, but I told him to let me know.

When I got into the house Sky was sprawled across my half of the bed, snoring gently in the faint glow from the streetlight outside. I stripped and nudged her leg and elbow out the way so that I could roll myself into the bed, and she grumbled something.

"How wazzt?" she added, slightly more awake.

"I was thinking of you."

Sky turned herself over and curled into me, one hand on my shoulder and her legs winding into mine. "I don't get why you like her."

"Boobs. Cunt. It's a job, really." I kissed her hair, enjoying the pre-warmed bed.

"I don't have boobs yet." She yawned, and then added, more awake, "Are you still going to like me when I have them?"

I ran my hand down her flat chest, tracing circles round a nipple. "Considering I like men and women, you definitely picked the right person to not worry about liking boobs."

"I worry," her quiet, tired voice said from my shoulder region.

I pulled her on top of me, and once we'd got elbows and legs sorted out and she was looking down at me, I said, "Sky, I love you however you look. I find you sexy now..." and I ran my hand down from her shoulder, across her smooth back and down to her ass, giving it a squeeze. "But I think I'm going to love it just as much when you have boobs and a cunt. I'm really looking forward to experimenting."

She was starting to smile. "It's going to take a long time."

"I know." I gave her ass a grope. "But that's fine. Look, I know you're not comfortable in this body, and that's cool. I love it, but I want you to be happy. And if that means you having an amazing rack and more toys for me to play with, then I'm all for it."

That definitely got a smile. "You're probably going to have to keep telling me that."

"Tell you that I find you sexy?" I rolled over, pinning her under me and looking down at her, smiling back up at me. "Oh, no. I'm going to show you."

Despite the previous orgasm, I was still horny. I fucked her slowly and gently, teasing her chest and nipples, running my hands down her legs. I told her what I'd do to her when she had boobs; told her that I'd put my cock between them and pinch her nipples, fucking her glorious round mounds while she played with herself, teasing her clit and dipping her fingers in and out of her cunt. I gripped her ass and followed its curve, wondering out loud how much it would grow, if she'd put on weight and curves, or if she'd have the same slim silhouette that I loved to bend over and fuck from behind. I wound my fingers into her hair and told her I'd still push her head to my cock and fuck her mouth until she'd smeared lipstick over my skin and her hair was messy and tangled. I wanted to see her in new clothes, breasts pushing a t-shirt out and tugging shirt buttons apart, knickers hiding a spray of hair and a wet, willing cunt. I wanted to lick and tease and play and make her moan—

She came in my hand, and then buried her face in the pillow. I pulled out, concern winning over desire. "Hey," I said, and wrapped myself around her, letting my erection subside. "Sky."

"Thank you." It was a bit muffled, and I think she was crying. "Thank you."

"I love you." It got easier every time I said it. "I'll love you however you look. And I'm gonna keep showing you that."

"Ok. Love you too."

I buried my face into the back of her neck, her hair against my cheek, and hugged her against me. I held her as she drifted off, her breathing settling into the quiet rhythm and then the gentle snores of earlier.

"I love you too," I told her quietly, and smiled to myself.

***

"Benny got the file from Tremain's," Sky reported to me as she hastily swallowed coffee the next morning. "So we don't have to ask two hundred people if Tanya Mardos threatened them."

"You only have to ask…"

"Ninety-three."

"Oh, for fuck's sake," I said. "There's got to be a better way to do this."

"Well, we know the people on the actual bid list did bid…" Sky said dubiously.

"Why not start with them, though. If I was her, I'd threaten everyone. The ones who bid, meaning they ignored her and might tell you what she offered. The ones who didn't bid, which meant they considered her enough of a threat to pull out."

Sky was staring at me, and then kissed me, hard.

"That's still…"

"Twenty-six people," Sky filled in.

"Better than ninety-three. Do you need me to do any of them?"

"No," Sky said. "The Queen doesn't want you involved. If any news gets back to Tanya, she'll know—she knows you work for the Queen. I could work for anyone."

I pulled her to me and hugged her. "I'm getting out."

My girlfriend smiled at me. "You just keep Tanya and Bear sweet, ok?"

"I'm working on it," I growled.

***

In between conversations, messages, drinks and speculation, I was still mindful of Bear's price. Our second date was scheduled for a week after the first, but it felt like only a few days when I arrived at the block of flats again. I got the lift, and Bear opened the door to me with a beaming smile.

As I entered, a woman stood up from where she was petting Bear's cat on the sofa; carefully styled brown hair, six-inch heels, a skirt that just grazed her kneecaps, and a suit jacket that concealed her boobs but emphasised the large wedge of cleavage. She gave me a pleased smile.

"Hi, Pol," I said, wondering what she was doing there.

"Hi, Nik."

And then we looked at each other.

"Pol wanted some fun." Bear stepped in. "So I thought we could provide that."

"What sort of fun?" I was feeling more uncomfortable about this by the second.

"Well, she suggested a threesome, and—"

"Ok, I'm going to stop you right there," I said, putting the bottle of wine I'd brought down on the counter. "I'm not cool with that."

Pol had raised both exquisitely shaped eyebrows at me. "I thought you were bisexual?"

"I am." I realised I'd folded my arms, and unfolded them. Cool. Casual. Just…work this out. "Bear, can I have a word? No offence, Pol."

"I'll freshen up," she said, giving me a smile that said she wasn't entirely sure what was going on, but would go along with it. We waited until she had closed the bathroom door, and then I turned to Bear.

"I thought you'd…" Bear was looking uncertain and upset

in equal measures. "Pol told me she wanted two men, and I know you fuck women, so…"

"Yeah." I was trying to find the words. "But you didn't ask me."

"You said you'd let me plan it. You were up for anything."

"No, I said I was happy to experiment. It's not that I don't want to fuck her, or you, or both." I was getting annoyed, and trying to find the words I needed. "It's about boundaries. My girlfriend agreed to a couple of dates with you, not you and someone else. She'd likely be fine with it but I want to check, and I don't want that conversation to be now, on the phone, while you wait. That's not fair to her."

Bear was still looking hurt, and I felt like a jerk. But… well, tough.

"Ok," he said after an uncomfortable silence. "So…"

"I'm going to head out." I tried a smile. "This just isn't my thing. I'm sure Pol's up for fun with you, though. She's a nice lady."

"Yeah." I saw the beard twitch in an equally awkward smile. "Yeah."

***

I walked away from the tower block feeling shitty, but also annoyed. I don't mind surprises, sure, but not when something like that is sprung on me. But…I'd turned down sex, and annoyed Bear.

I huffed, and shoved my hands into my pockets. Well. Given the choice between fucking Pol and pissing Sky off…I'd go with not pissing off the woman I loved.

Sky was out when I got back and I found Jim in the kitchen, eating pasta. He glanced up at me, and said, "Alcohol in the fridge."

"Does it show?"

"Yeah."

I got myself a bottle and sat opposite him at the small table.

"Date not go well?" Jim's a fastidious eater, and laid his fork carefully on the side of his plate while he talked.

"He tried to spring a threesome on me."

"Don't you like threesomes?"

"I've never had one for pleasure," I said, and took a swig of the bottle. "I definitely don't like them when I'm not asked. And I haven't asked Sky."

"I didn't think you were tied to her apron strings—"

I think my glare withered him in his tracks. We had a moment of silence, and then I said, "Part of the deal of Sky trusting me enough to sleep with other people is that I don't abuse that trust. I let her know that I was going on dates with Bear. If I suddenly fuck someone else, that's not part of the deal. She'll be fine with it, but…" I tried to think of an analogy that would get it through to him. "It's like someone giving you a job, then suddenly changing the deal. You could do it, but you wouldn't be happy."

I saw something slowly cross his face, and hoped it was understanding. "I see."

"Yeah?"

"Changing the job." Jim nodded, and picked up his fork again.

"And I hope," I said to the dapper man across the table, who had just stabbed a piece of pasta exactly in the middle, "that you'll cut the sexist bullshit next time anyone brings the subject up."

We locked gazes. And then Jim gave me another nod, and returned to his pasta. I took my alcohol bottle into the living room to find a sofa and something shit on TV, and tried to ignore both my irritation and my thwarted sex drive.

***

It was 11pm when my phone rang, just as I was in the middle of some episode of a drama. I picked it up, winced at the caller name, and then decided I was tipsy enough to handle taking it. "Yeah?"

"*Hi. Um. It's Bear. So, um.*"

"Take your time." I flicked the phone onto speaker and put it on the table, flopping myself back onto the sofa and waiting for Bear to get his thoughts in line.

"*Pol explained it.*" There was a silence, and then he said, "*Well, she tore me a new one. She thought I'd asked you, and you'd agreed. She didn't realise I hadn't.*"

I couldn't help laughing. "She's pretty persuasive when she's angry, isn't she."

"*The heels didn't help,*" Bear admitted, laughing as well. I relaxed. If he was laughing then that meant he wasn't too pissed with me. "*She did some explaining, and I'm sorry. I didn't think it through, and…and it was real jerk move. I should have asked you beforehand.*"

"I just don't like that sort of surprise. It's not just about me, you know?"

"*Yeah. I was thinking with my dick.*"

"Hey, I don't usually have a problem with that."

He chuckled. "*So, um. Can I restart?*"

"Sure."

237

"Ok, I've had an offer from a nice lady. She wants a threesome with two dicks, and I immediately thought of you."

I laughed. "Thanks, man."

"So, how about it? Can you check with Sky and let me know if you'd be up for that?"

"Sure I can. She's not in so it's not tonight—"

"Nah, nah, that's cool. Pol's gone home anyway."

"Ok. I'll let you know."

"If you're not up for it then let me know, and…we'll find something else to do?"

"Yeah. That'd be fun. Thanks for calling."

"That's…that's ok. I'm sorry for being a dick."

"Happy to be one when Pol's concerned."

He laughed. I hung up the phone and smiled at the ceiling.

Well, that hadn't gone too badly. And a threesome with Pol? That could be fun.

***

And it was.

I returned a couple of evenings later to find Pol sitting at the bar, enjoying a selection of Bear's cooking. I joined her happily as Bear added a few more platefuls, and the chef then proceeded to regale Pol with what he'd done to me on our previous date.

Now, I don't blush easily, but…well. Hearing it from someone else's lips was pretty hot.

Pol immediately wanted to try it. Bear obliged by sliding a piece of melon between her lips, but then admitted that he had other things he wanted to try.

"Oh?" Pol asked archly.

"Well, you know. Two men." He was starting to go red. "I think there's more exciting things than using you as a plate."

"Where do you want me?" Pol asked, in a good imitation of Tanya's tiger purr.

"Well…" Bear said.

I'd already moved a plate, and was bending her forward over the counter. Pol went willingly, kneeling up on the stool until her stomach was on the counter and reaching for Bear's zip.

"I…hadn't exactly…" the chef said, and then Pol had his erect cock out and into her mouth. I saw his eyes widen above the beard, and he groaned.

"I want to play, Pol," I said, running my hand in circles on her ass. "Can I?"

I got a definitely agreeable noise, muffled by Bear's cock, and I began to slide Pol's skirt up. Her hands came down to help me pull the fabric out of the way and then I could slide my fingers up and down her ass, circling her hole and trailing down to her cunt. Bear was obviously appreciating the noises she was making, and groaned as the vibrations hummed against his cock.

I slid two fingers into Pol's wet cunt, finger-fucking her as she spread her legs wider for me. She tugged her head back from Bear's cock for a moment, and looked up at him. "Fuck my mouth."

"Oh." I'm not sure Bear had ever been asked to do that before. He wound his hand into Pol's hair, and began—gingerly—to do as she asked.

"You can go pretty hard," I told him, busy at the other end, playing with Pol's clit as I fucked her with my other

239

hand.

"Oh. Ok." He thrust harder, and by the noises Pol was making, she certainly did like it.

I knew from prior comments—not experience, I haven't fucked every one of Hensch's toys—that Pol was quite hard to bring to orgasm, and so I wasn't surprised when her hand snaked down and slid under her legs. I left her to finger her clit and focused on sliding another finger into her cunt, fucking her with four. She was taking it, bucking back against me, and it looked like she was deep-throating Bear's cock. Certainly he was pushing hard against her, his face set in concentration.

"Oh…" he said, and almost doubled over. "Oh. Fuck. Yes."

Pol's fingers were moving quickly, and I could feel her cunt clenching around my fingers. I pushed in deeper, getting my knuckles in, and she moaned, jerking against me as she came.

Wow, she had strong muscles. I relaxed my hand—she'd probably have broken my fingers, otherwise—and waited it out. She was damn sexy, bent over the table.

Bear levered himself upright and Pol wriggled. I carefully eased my hand out, looking at the shining fluid she'd left all over it. "You ok, Pol?"

"Just peachy, darling." She slid herself off the worktop and smiled at me, her lips and chin coated in saliva and her eyes bright. "Nothing like an orgasm to wake a girl up. What next? You haven't come yet."

"Nope." I went round to wash my hand, squeezing Bear's ass on the way. "What's the next plan, maestro?"

"Another?" He grinned, despite the quick breaths he was taking. "I want to fuck you, Pol. Can you cope with two of us?"

"You know how to fuck an ass, Nikolas?" Pol said.

I turned from drying my hands, and rolled my eyes at her. "You've met my girlfriend, right?"

"She's adorable. You're behind," Pol told me. "Bear, get your kit off and get the condoms."

Five minutes later, Bear was on the sofa, completely naked apart from a condom. Pol swung her leg over his hips and leant forward over him, rubbing her breasts against his hairy chest. "You can go hard, Nikolas."

"Old habits," I grumbled, and put myself behind her, over Bear's legs. I had the bottle of lube in one hand, and squeezed some onto a finger. "How about…"

Wow, she was fast. She opened her ass up to me, swallowing my finger.

"So, uh, I can fuck you?" I asked, and picked up the condom.

"Let me just get settled on Bear."

The man under us groaned as Pol slid onto his cock, and then she bent forward and kissed him. I took the opportunity to add some more lube to her ass, and then I was sliding my cock in, filling her.

Being inside her with Bear's cock was a whole new sensation. I could feel him pressing against me, a pressure against the front of my cock that wasn't normally there—and then Pol started touching herself, and…just wow. Everything tensed, and it was almost overwhelming.

"Stay with me, Nikolas," Pol murmured, and began to

move. I had to grab her hips to stay inside, and I could feel Bear's cock sliding, again and again. It felt—so—good—

And I came, thrusting into Pol, my hands tight on her hips, my forehead resting on her smooth back. "Oh, fuck. Fuck."

"It's ok. Stay in," Pol said, still moving. Bear was panting underneath her.

"I'm too sensitive," I admitted, panting and frustrated. I'd wanted to last longer. Fuck!

"That's ok, hun. Got a plug?"

Bear had left one on the table, and so I slid my too-sensitive cock out and replaced it with the plug. Pol started moving again, and I got to watch Bear's face from the side. I sat myself on the floor and played with his nipples, pinching and sucking, kissing his neck and his ear and his mouth—

Pol moaned and swore, but she kept moving even as she came. Bear was so close, I could see it.

And my hand on his balls was all that was needed to push him over the edge, frowning and gasping in something that was almost pain.

We just sat there for a bit, letting the sensations fade.

"Everything you wanted?" Pol said to Bear as she slid herself off, making him wince.

"Well, I dunno…" The grin on his face belied the words. "You might have to come back sometime."

Chapter Six

So what's happening?" I asked Sky and the Queen. It was far too early in the morning for me—by which I mean it was before midday—and we were back in the Queen's headquarters. I was drinking coffee, and trying to work out what was going on.

"Everything's still ongoing," the Queen said blandly.

"That's not very helpful."

"Did you find out anything useful?"

"Not really," I said. "Although word on the street says the Angels have pulled their investigation into the Mardos'. Possibly blackmail."

"Can't we…" Sky started.

"Look," I said impatiently, not wanting her to drop me in anything, "if rumours are true and she is blackmailing someone into closing down their current investigation, what do you think the odds of getting another one into Tanya Mardos for the auction blackmail are likely to be? We don't have any details or any information to give them. It'll just get blocked again. We're better off staying out of it."

"I disagree," the Queen said calmly. "I would appreciate knowing what is going on, and you're going to find out for me, Nikolas."

"All right," I grumbled. If the Queen had ordered me, at least it wouldn't look too suspicious…and I wanted to know who Tanya had fingered too. "I'll look into it further."

"And in the meantime?" Sky said. "We stick with plan A: get the information on Mardos, dump it on everyone?"

"That works," the Queen said. "Sky, you're still investigating our leads. Has your hacker provided the documents?"

"I'll get what we have over to you. Have you got anything?"

"Enough," the Queen said. "Bear has been helpful too. We have a good deal of information on three cases, and more circumstantial information on another six. It should be sufficient."

"When are you pushing this to…anyone?" I asked.

"To the police as soon as we decide who will be most receptive," the Queen said briskly. "Media outlets and… selected people…whenever we have everything ready. It will take a day to finish wrapping everything up. I want to get it in before they decide to move against me."

"If you give the police all this, the mole could try to take you out," I warned.

"I'm expecting it." She leaned back. "I need to know who's

going to cause the most amount of trouble, and who Tanya has been bribing. Get me names, Nikolas."

***

"You could try asking Sam about your mole," Sky said as we walked away from the pub. "You know her dirty little secret."

"Doesn't mean I'd spill it," I grumbled.

"She doesn't know that. I don't mind if you indulge her if that'd help."

"I'm just not sure puppy play is my thing, Sky. I mean, she's cute, but...the ears? A tail? Really?"

Sky giggled. "A tail's just a butt plug. Try it and see. It's not something I'm into, so it might be your only chance."

"You wouldn't wear ears?" She was still giggling and I grabbed two handfuls of her hair, pushing them up into knots over her ears. "You'd look cute with ears."

"See, maybe you are into it." She gave me a long, lingering kiss, and then extracted her hair—and herself—from me. "Give it a try."

I sighed. The club it was, then.

I arranged things with Hensch, and took myself back to the club the next evening. The downstairs bar was the kind of tacky stripper scene that I wasn't really into—there's only so many jollies I can get looking when I can't touch—and I was glad to be let through the door into the private area. If nothing else, it was quieter...albeit filled with more leather and cocks than you'd normally see at a strip club. I took the chair offered by the fox-tail and looked around as he got me a drink. Everyone was chilled out, and that was nice. It was an eclectic and weird mix, but I liked it. I liked being fully dressed, too. I saw how people looked at me: I was in control. I could see how that sort of feeling could be intoxicating.

As I was absently musing on that, the server in the fox tail approached. "Excuse me, sir?"

He was waiting for permission, so I nodded.

"The couple there would like to involve you in a scene." He gestured at a couple on the far side of the room—a clean-shaven, round-faced man with a mop of brown hair, and another portlier man by his feet, dressed in a cock sheath, ears, and I suspected a tail. One man and his dog.

The mop-haired man was chatting to a woman next to him who appeared to be clothed in scraps of leather, but the dog was watching me.

"What does that involve?" I asked the server.

"Bruno is a bad dog, sir. You just need to make a fuss of him so that his owner can apologise and then punish him…in front of you, if you'd like."

"No fucking?"

"You don't even have to take your clothes off, sir."

I shrugged. Well, of all the requests I've had, it wasn't the weirdest. "Sure. I don't mind people fucking in front of me."

"I will pass that on, sir."

About ten minutes later, I was chatting to a denim-clad older man about business (his) when I felt a rub against my knee. It was the dog-man, his ears perched on his head, looking up at me with bright eyes. He did have a tail, curled up over his back.

I switched my drink to my other hand and entertained the brief flash of doubt about how on earth I'd got myself into this weird situation. It was a man. Human skin and face and all that. Kneeling on all fours, wearing ears and a butt-plug, and not much else…pretending to be a dog. What. The. Fuck.

But as I gave the base of one of his dog ears a scratch, I shoved the weirdness away. It was fantasy, wasn't it? Same as we all do; just some of us turn up the swagger and walk into bars, and some of us get to put on dog ears and act cute to strangers for scratches. It's whatever gets you off.

So I gave his ears a scratch and told him he was a cute boy. He managed to wag his tail pretty convincingly, and tried to lick my face while I scratched under his chin. By the way the cock sheath was wagging he was enjoying the interaction in his own way, so I just focused on being nice to the cute dog that was being friendly…

Until his owner turned up.

"I'm so sorry, is he being a nuisance?" It was the mop-haired man, holding a collar. "Bruno, heel."

The dog ignored him, and continued wagging his tail at me.

"Bruno!"

The dog gave his 'owner' a look, but I switched my petting to his ears again and he turned back. May as well give him a reason to be punished…

The mop-haired man clipped the collar around Bruno's neck with an annoyed look, and dragged him away from my leg. "I'm so sorry, sir. Was he any trouble?"

I waved an uncaring hand. "He's a cute mutt."

The man gave me a smile. "He is. When he's not being bad." That turned into a glare at the dog now giving an apologetic look up, trying to look cute and waiting for the words…

"You're a bad dog."

The flinch was pretty good, but I saw the cock sheath twitch.

"If I tell you to come, you come."

The cock sheath gave a definite twitch there, and I wondered about the double meaning of the words. It sounded like that was part of the game.

The dog was whining and grovelling, and I found myself getting weirdly wrapped up in it. It was obviously a scene they'd played out before, with variations; I wondered if the bad behaviour changed, and the punishment. It was obvious that the conclusion wouldn't.

There was a tap on my arm just as the 'owner' was pulling out his dog's butt-plug, ready to have his pleasure with his pet. I turned and found Pol there.

"Honey!" She kissed my cheek, and then gestured down. "What do you think of my new pet? Isn't she just the cutest? She's new, quite shy. Give her a pat."

It was Sam; butt-naked apart from a pair of ears buried in her dark, curly hair, a butt-plug in the shape of a tail that curved up over her back, and a collar around her neck that led to the leash Pol was holding. She raised her eyes to mine, that dark flush spreading over her cheeks. Wow, she'd definitely taken to the kink quite fast, but hey, if it suited her...

I put my drink down and held out a hand, palm-down, thinking of how I'd normally approach shy dogs. "Here, girl. What's her name?"

"Sam," Pol said, smirking at me. Sam crawled forward and sniffed my hand, so I gave her ears a scratch. The curly hair did feel good, and I felt my cock stir. It would feel amazing under my fingers. Ok, maybe I would be ok with this...

Pol sat herself down on the footstool opposite me, and said, "Sit." Sam obediently folded herself up by Pol's feet, between us. I kept scratching her ears, and then moved to under her chin as Pol and I chatted. And weirdly, it felt natural. It was like having an odd-shaped dog, but I realised I'd gotten over the awkwardness of thinking it was a human. I mean, Sam was, but...

"I think she likes you," Pol said, as Sam rolled over to have her belly scratched. I leant down to stroke the smooth skin: she had her paws in the air, tongue out, hips moving as she wagged her tail. "You can fuck her if you want."

"I think that'd feel a bit weird," I admitted.

"Well, I'll leave her with you for a moment if that's ok. I need to go talk to someone."

"Uh, sure." I accepted the lead, and Sam rolled over and sat down again, her chin resting on my knee, staring up adoringly. I scratched her ears, and then said, "Um. Look, I needed to talk to you about...business. I need—"

I stopped because of the look on Sam's face. It had gone from adoring-puppy to confused, and was now approaching upset human. Shit.

"I'm sorry, I didn't..."

She almost snatched the lead out of my hand, and got up off her knees. I half-stood as she headed for the door to the back rooms, sure that I'd seen tears. Fuck, fuck, fuck.

Pol had caught sight of it too, and was already heading in that direction. She gave me a look that very accurately conveyed "what the fuck have you done this time," along with "stay right where you are", and so I sank back into my seat.

I'd got through the rest of my drink and was wondering if

I should leave when Pol returned. She sat down on the footstool and gave me a look.

"I fucked up?" I asked.

"You fucked up. When someone's playing, Nik, you don't break character. You get what I'm saying?"

"I should have stuck with puppy?"

"You should have stuck with puppy. She's pretty upset."

"I only asked…"

"You wouldn't have a conversation with a dog."

"I wouldn't fuck a dog!" I gestured behind her to where there was indeed a fuck-session going on.

"She's someone different here. We all are. Don't talk work!" Pol was glaring at me. "I know you do with Hensch, but that's different. This is his work."

I sighed, exasperated. "I don't get it."

"Well, she's back in human persona now, so if you wanted to ask something you may as well come and do it." Pol stalked off towards the back rooms, and I followed.

Sam was sitting on a chair, surrounded by rails of leather and silk and assorted stacks of boxes. She was still sniffing, but was dressed in a fluffy robe and had taken her ears and collar off. Pol shoved me through the door and said, "I'm right outside when you want to get rid of him, hun."

Sam nodded, and tried a wobbly smile at me.

"I'm sorry," I told her, sitting down on one of the other chairs. "Pol…tried to explain. I don't really get it but…I didn't mean to."

Sam just shrugged. "What did you want?"

"I need some police information. Someone's blocked the investigation into Tanya Mardos, and I want to know who.

Possibly why as well, but I don't think you'll find out."

She nodded. "Ok. I can do that."

"Do you..." I sighed. "Can I do anything? What can I say that's going to make it better?"

She looked at her hands. "No. I'm going to go home now anyway."

"Just don't fuck up again." Pol had opened the door behind me. "You want him out, hun?"

Sam looked up and tried another smile. "It's ok. I'll go shower."

"I'll see myself out," I told Pol, and headed past her. Pol shut the door on Sam and stopped me with a hand on my arm.

"It's probably not permanent," she said, "but give it a while. A couple of weeks, maybe. She's still getting into this."

I nodded. "I'll meet her someplace normal next time."

The brunette sighed, and gave me a kiss on the cheek. "You're an idiot, Nik. Sometimes I think you've got it, and then you go and do something stupid."

"I do try," I protested.

"I know you do." She shook her head. "Idiot."

***

That evening, I was over at Bear's. It was sort of a last-minute date, but I didn't have any problem with that. We were going to fuck, and we both had our clothes off almost as soon as I stepped through the door.

"I want to fuck you," Bear said, taking a momentary break from kissing my neck and tugging me towards the centre of the room. "On your knees. I want to fuck you on the table."

"You are so hot," I commented, kneeling down in front of

the table. It had a few bits on it, and I mentally catalogued how much damage they'd do if we knocked them off. Remotes, not much…should be fine. The cat opened one lazy eye at me from the sofa, decided I was boring, and went back to sleep. Well, that suited me.

Bear pushed me down and then slid my hands up until I was gripping the top edge, my cheek against the cool wood. "Stay there," he growled, and I felt the head of his cock nudge my ass. I moaned and spread my legs, wanting him.

He filled me with a slow stroke, one hand on my hip and the other running up and down my back. The table was exactly the right height to take my weight and I spread my legs further, letting my hands rest over my head. Bear pressed one hand against my neck, pinning me against the table, and filled me with one hard stroke that made me groan.

And then he stopped.

"Oh, fuck…" I was trying to move but he was pinning me, his weight gently bearing down on the back of my neck and his hips pushing mine into the table. I was naked, rock-hard, and desperate to be fucked. "Please…"

"I've got something I need to say," Bear's low growl said into my ear.

Danger.

Every sense sprang alert. I was in possibly the most unfortunate position to be able to do anything; I could break out, sure, but it would hurt Bear. It could come to that…but I'd see what he wanted first.

"Nikolas…" Bear said. "Detective."

I couldn't help it. I'm an accomplished liar, but not when I'm bent naked over a table with another man's cock filling my ass. I know I tensed.

I was in serious, serious trouble.

"I'm not going to turn you in," Bear said quickly, I guess trying to forestall any sudden moves on my part. "I've known for a while."

"All right." I managed to keep my voice relatively calm. His hand was still on the back of my neck, and I couldn't turn my head to look at him. "So?"

I felt his body bend over mine, warm skin rubbing against my back. His breath was warm in my ear. "I want a favour from you."

"I'm not in any position to say no, am I?" It came out rather more bitter than I'd intended. I'd been having a nice time, and he'd brought work into it...well, now I knew how Sam felt when I'd brought work into her puppy-time. I'm an idiot sometimes.

All right, most of the time. Especially when I let myself get pinned down and into trouble.

"You want to safeword?" Bear asked, his voice low and serious.

And just like that, I was hard again. He knew about my allegiance, sure, but we were still playing. I knew that trouble and danger get me off, but I'd never experienced it so close at hand, and not combined in such a way. I was suddenly very, very turned on. "What's the favour?"

His warmth and weight lifted off me, and then his hands were spreading my butt-cheeks and he slowly pushed his cock deeper, right to the hilt. It was almost painful, and I could hear my own ragged breathing.

"You're moving against all of us." His cock was slowly

withdrawing, taking that sensation of fullness with it. I waited to see what he'd do. "So I want immunity."

His cock was sliding in again, a little faster, and I pushed back against it. I wanted it.

"Naughty," Bear said, and paused for a moment with his cock in to the hilt.

"Come on," I told him. Begged him. "Fuck me."

"I want something from you."

"Just fuck me. Please." I wanted him to move. I needed it.

"I want immunity."

"I can't—" I started, and he pulled out, pushed back in. Oh, fuck, that was good. "I can't give you—" Another stroke. "Bear, I'm not—"

He fucked me through my ragged denials and half-made phrases, jumbled together in a mess of want and pleasure. The table was firm under me, the surface slick with my sweat, and my fingers were aching from gripping the edge, but I didn't care. He was holding my hips and fucking me, and I didn't want it to end.

"Give it to me," Bear said as I jerked and writhed.

"I can't."

"Nikolas."

"I don't have—"

"Tell me."

"I don't...I don't...oh god, please..." My orgasm was building, and I was lost as he thrust in again and again and then one final time, so deep that it pushed me over the edge. I could feel my cock pulsing out into nothing, a release so desperate and overwhelming I think I blacked out.

"Nikolas, c'mon." It was Bear's voice, gentle and worried.

"Stand up, c'mon, slowly. Here."

I felt light-headed, my legs wobbly. He put one arm under me and almost lifted me across to one of the sofas, pushing me down onto the cushions. "Stay still. I'll get you a drink."

He was still naked, I realised, as he came back with a glass.

"I think I'm too good," he said with a laugh as he sat down on the edge of the sofa next to my hip, although he still looked pretty worried. "How are you feeling?"

"Ok." I didn't risk sitting up yet. "That was...intense."

"I was a bit worried."

I took a sip of the water and then looked him in the eye. "Don't ever do that again. Not to me, not to anyone."

"I thought you'd run away."

"Well, yeah." I gave him a long stare. "You're a dangerous man, and you just told me you know I'm working for people you don't like. I don't want to be around someone who might...y'know, kneecap me."

Bear was starting to look embarrassed again. "I fucked up again, didn't I?" he muttered.

"Yeah."

"I'm sorry."

"Do you get me, though?" I was starting to shake, and not from the effects of the orgasm.

"You could have safeworded."

"I didn't know that until you said."

The big man scratched his beard and looked away. "Yeah. Ok. Um. Jeez, I fucked up. But...you enjoyed it."

I leaned my head back and let out a breath, trying to make my body relax. "I get off on danger, but that's definitely not everyone's thing. Just don't do it to anyone else. It was a dick move."

He nodded.

"As for your favour…I can't do what you want. I'm just a field detective, I don't have any power. I can punt it to my boss but I can't promise you anything."

Bear leaned over and gently kissed my lips. His mouth tasted of salt and hops. "What's going to happen?"

"Seriously, I don't know." I felt wrung out. "I just get the information. I pass it up. I'm not involved in any of the policy or decisions." I put my glass down on the table and added, "If it was up to me, I'd be hammering Tanya fucking Mardos, not you guys."

"Why can't you?"

I shook my head. "There isn't much I can do when the higher-ups are blocking me."

"Fine. Then we'll get her in our own way." Bear's face had snapped into a more serious mode. "We're doing this."

"Right now?"

He immediately gave a rueful smile. "Nah. Right now, I'm getting you a hot drink, and we're going to chill for a bit until you can walk again."

"I dunno," I said, testing my legs. "I owe you an orgasm. I think both of our legs might be having issues when we're done."

Chapter Seven

Knowing that Bear had somehow found out, I expected the worst when the Queen asked to see me the next morning. I walked into the pub and then down to her office, wondering if it would be a bullet to the brain...no, that was melodramatic. If she knew, she'd want a plea bargain too.

And I was right.

"At least Bear gave me an orgasm while he asked," my mouth said before my brain could get involved.

"That could be arranged." Nothing fazes the Queen. "Boy? Girl? Both?"

I waved a hand. "Neither. I was being snarky. What do you want specifically?"

"As much of this left intact as possible," the Queen said, waving a hand around. "My organisation isn't the one you should be interested in."

I sighed. "I'll tell you the same thing I told him. I'm a field detective. I can punt it up to my boss, but I don't have any authority to demand anything. It'd be up to them."

The Queen nodded.

"You could…" I thought about it. "Dump the information anonymously?"

"It's not about that. I know you've been working on us for a while, along with that bitch." The Queen leaned back. "So when I found out I decided to put you to good use. I needed someone to root out the bad seeds, and I'd rather have that done legally. It saves my finding places to bury the bodies."

I wasn't really surprised that she'd been using me to do her dirty work. "You could have said."

"Then you wouldn't have done what I wanted," the Queen returned. "But after a year, surely your organisation must have enough information. If they move against that bitch they'll be forced to move against me too, and you know that I'm better than she is. I'll help your lot against her, in exchange for immunity."

"I'll offer the suggestion." Privately, I suspected that my bosses would go for that: or at least if they had any sense, they would. But hey, I was just a field agent. "I'm likely to get arrested too, though. I've been working for you."

The Queen favoured me with a smile. "That did throw me off the scent for a while. A police detective who's willing to get his hands dirty?"

I shrugged, but smiled back. "That's the fun bit. Oh, I have a name for you."

The Queen raised her eyebrows. "The police mole?"

"Yeah." Sam had somehow come through. "Although…

258

usual disclaimers." I still didn't know who had set Sam to trail me, or why I'd suddenly come under enough suspicion to warrant a tail at that point. She nodded, and I slid the scrap of paper over the desk.

"Well, we'll investigate," the Queen said once she'd read it. "But I don't think it's relevant now. We've got everything we need."

***

It was three days later when I caught the shadow out of the window.

I'd got up and put coffee on. I heard Sky walk down the hall towards the shower, and ambled over towards the window to check the weather. Not too bad, a bit grey—

Someone standing across the road.

Now, I'm a sneaky bugger. I stood at just the wrong angle to be seen, but where I could spot whoever was watching the front door...

And someone was.

Hmm.

I went back to the coffee and thoughtfully made a mug, and then made a second to leave for Sky when she came out of the shower.

Then I refilled the coffee pot and put it on again.

Milk, sugar, another sugar, and then I took a swig and headed back towards the window. A young-ish man, playing on his phone. There would likely be someone else at the back, too...

I went and checked the window in Jim's room, but there wasn't anyone to be seen in the yard or over the fence. They'd definitely be cutting off escape routes, though.

I considered running—ok, well, heading out in an entirely normal fashion and then running like hell—but I also knew it wouldn't help. Someone would be tailing me, and I'd be leaving Sky. May as well let them get it over with and see what the fallout was…

And so, when the knock came at the door, I opened it four seconds later.

"Good morning," I said evenly to the officer in front of me, and then eyeballed Sam, a bit more dressed than I'd previously seen her. "Come on in. Coffee?"

"No, thank you," the officer said, stepping in.

"Is Sky around?" Sam asked, managing to sound composed.

"She's just…" I heard the shower switch off. "Getting a shower. She'll be out in a minute."

"Mr Jinsen, it is my duty to inform you…"

"That I'm under arrest, I know. Come and have tea while you give me the rest of the speech."

They did have tea while we waited for Sky, and chatted about life at the station; despite the fact they were supposed to be arresting me, we were at least civilised about it.

Then Sky appeared, drying her hair. "I'll just get my shoes on."

We bagged a lift to the station from the officers, and as we left the flat, I noticed the lurker had vanished. Well, other jobs to move on to…I wondered absently what would have happened if I'd run. They'd have tried to catch up, sure, but…

I would have left Sky.

Or she could have come with me?

That could have been fun.

We arrived at the station, stood around while they completed the formalities, and then Sam escorted us to a cell. I kept an eye on her for any signal, but she was entirely straight-faced as she ushered us into the small, bare room.

Well, I'd just have to wait and see.

Sky knew better than to ask anything, but settled down next to me on the bench and slid her hand into mine.

And then we waited.

***

"I know the theory for this," Sky said an hour later. "What if it doesn't work?"

"We talk to a lawyer and worry about it all then," I told her. I was lying on the bench, enjoying the chance to have a brief nap, and she was absently pacing the room. "We'll find out when someone turns up at the door."

It ended up being Sam who turned up.

I sat up on the bench, and Sky turned, the picture of elegance.

Sam opened the door, and held it. "You're being released."

"Not that I'm objecting," I said as we walked out past her, "by why?"

"Lack of evidence," Sam said, flat and official.

I wasn't about to look a gift horse in the mouth. Sky and I left.

"Do you think the Queen's been taken in?" Sky asked.

"We can go find out."

The pub was closed, which said enough. Sky and I stared at the door, and then turned. "Bear?" I wondered absently.

"He'll have stayed out of it," Sky said with certainty.

I texted, and got a return a few seconds later. Well, at least that was one person who was fine. And Tanya?

Sky just shrugged. "I don't think there's any way you can safely find out until it's announced."

"Home, then?"

Sky considered. "I can't think of any place better."

***

Two days later, I found myself in the strip club. It was out of hours, but I didn't mind. I wasn't here to play. There were a few dancers hanging around, mostly clothed, so it wasn't too weird.

Sam was waiting in the back room, fully dressed, sipping something. She looked a lot more at ease than when I'd first met her, even without her tail and ears.

"So?" I asked, sitting down.

"You're an operative, so they're not charging you," Sam said. "Or Sky, because there's no evidence against her."

I'd counted on Sky either being classed as an operative or small fry, whichever got her out from under the radar. And it sounded like that had worked. "Coke, thanks," I said to the fox-tail who came to take my order. "Did you get the police mole?"

"She got swept up with the rest," Sam said. "There was some nasty blackmail. The Queen's turned evidence, so she's not even looking at a prison sentence."

"Good." I was glad to know that my arrangement there had gone through, at least. "Did you pick up Bear?"

She frowned, trying to remember. "No charges. No evidence. The information on the Jacks wasn't in the files—I only knew about it because I knew you'd got it originally."

I had to laugh. They'd been one step ahead of me. "Oh

well." I took the drink that the fox-tail brought over. "And Tanya?"

Sam grinned. "There's enough evidence for it to go to trial."

I raised my glass.

"She could still get off," Sam warned.

I shrugged. "That's the legal's problem, not mine." And it would do what the Queen wanted: smear the bitch beyond any hope of a political career.

"Are you staying here?" Sam asked.

"I'm not sure," I admitted. "I was thinking of travelling anyway. Is that a hint?"

The police officer made a face. "No, but…she blackmailed enough people. If she thinks you're involved…"

"True. I'll think about it. Did you get the promotion?"

"It's in the works."

I leaned forward. "I want to say thanks. I know you put in testimony on the files, and it meant the charges got dropped. Thank you."

She was going red, that wonderful spreading blush that I liked. "You…helped me."

I glanced around the room, seeing the mostly-naked waiter in his fox tail, the odd assortment of chairs and furniture, the tables and straps. Then I looked back at Sam, neat in her suit and slicked-back curls that desperately wanted to escape and curl around her dog-ears. "If this makes you happy, then I'm all for that. You're a cute puppy, Sam."

She smiled. "Well. Yeah. Thanks." If she had her tail in, I think she would have wagged it.

***

I found Sky outside the strip club, leaning against the wall, waiting for me. I wound an arm around her shoulders, and we headed back towards my flat.

"So," I asked, "how about travelling?"

"Is that an official warning?" she asked.

"No, just something to consider." I twisted a strand of her hair around my finger. "You could be Storm, you know, like when you dyed your hair grey before. And if you had your surgery, you'd be someone else." She was looking thoughtful, so I added, "You've got the money now. You could take some time to recover, and then go see some of the world."

"What would you do?"

"I've had jobs offers in a couple of cities, and Bear's offered me some work if I want it. Plus, I've just had some bonuses come in. I've got the money to travel."

She was considering it. "Being away from here for a bit could be good. I'd like to travel."

"I could have sex with you in every city on the planet. How's that for aims?"

She raised her eyebrows. "Every city? That could take a while."

"I've got time. Ever joined the mile high club?"

"No." She sounded thoughtful. "I've never had sex on a beach, either."

I wound my arm around her shoulders as hers came around my waist. "Well. I guess we'd better get started then, shouldn't we?"

The beautiful woman beside me smiled up. "Places to go, people to fuck…"

I smiled back down at her as we walked off, down the pavement, into the anonymity of the city. "Exactly."

ABOUT THE AUTHOR

Ellie Barker mostly writes short'n'dirty flash fiction and short erotic fiction in any genre going. She prefers vampires over werewolves, and is always hot for a rainy night.

You can find out more about Ellie at:

http://elliebarker.co.uk

OTHER SINFUL PRESS TITLES

PEEPER by SJ Smith
BY MY CHOICE by Christine Blackthorn
SHOW ME, SIR by Sonni de Soto
THE HOUSE OF FOX by SJ Smith
A VARIETY OF CHAINS by Christine Blackthorn
IN BONDS OF THE EARTH by Janine Ashbless
THE LIBERTINE DIARIES by Isabella Delmonico
SINFUL PLEASURES - An Anthology of Erotic Tales
THE PRISON OF THE ANGELS by Janine Ashbless
NAMED AND SHAMED by Janine Ashbless
FIERCE ENCHANTMENTS by Janine Ashbless
MAKING HIM WAIT by Kay Jaybee

For more information about Sinful Press
please visit
www.sinfulpress.co.uk

Lightning Source UK Ltd.
Milton Keynes UK
UKHW01f1555120718
325611UK00001B/2/P